Rescue from the Rose

This is a story of love and murder set in a fashionable watering-place in provincial England just before the First World War. It evokes in affectionate and imaginative detail a landscape that was still predominantly rural and peoples it with characters utterly alive and convincing within their time; and torn by conflicts and passions.

It is around the public house called the *Little Rose* that the life of an isolated community revolves. And it is, or seems to be, around the beautiful girl, Miriam Bennett, that the life of the *Little Rose* revolves. Miriam is a splendid barmaid, a useful servant in the daily offices of the pub. She is also a focus for men, and for trouble.

Within the clear outlines of this powerful story a number of intriguing and eccentric characters are developed in depth. The clash between them leads logically to the drama—and successful melodrama—of the narrative.

Hangman's Tide by this author did well, and so did his *No Birds Sang*. But in *Rescue from the Rose* he breaks entirely new ground, with a murder plot set in recent provincial history and a story that is taut, exciting and marvellously aware of the slow pulse of the Derbyshire countryside, the circumscribed passions of the people who used to live there.

RESCUE
FROM THE ROSE

JOHN BUXTON HILTON

BOOK CLUB ASSOCIATES
LONDON

This edition published 1976 by
Book Club Associates
by arrangement with Macmillan London Limited

Printed in Great Britain by
NORTHUMBERLAND PRESS LIMITED
Gateshead

*Another
for
Rebecca*

CHAPTER ONE

In the winter of 1911, the High Peak of Derbyshire lay in the grip of a cold spell such as Alice Bonsall had not known since the unforgettable weeks before Jonty was born. Great ploughs had been out in the streets. The biggest of them, drawn by five horses, had struggled up to Higher Buxton pushing great wedges of snow on to the edges of the pavements. Frozen ruts lay parallel and lifeless along every street. Milk was frozen in the roundsman's can. Icicles as long and thick as a man's leg hung from gutters broken and overhanging from the weight they bore. A horse stumbled and fell in the High Street and had to be shot where it lay, the crimson stain mute and horrifying in the surrounding drifts for nearly a month afterwards.

It was cold in the train in which Alice and Jonathan waited to be drawn down the frozen Dale. Motionless and huddled they sat in opposite corner seats, waiting for the engine to be shunted on that would send warming steam through the pipes under their seats. Alice had her hands in a fur muff, clasping a hand-warmer, a leather-covered metal tube packed with smouldering charcoal. It brought a little life and feeling to the tips of her fingers, but could do nothing to abate her larger shivers. Jonathan took a mouthful of whisky from a flask that had once been the property of one of the General's guests—it was surprising how many little objects changed hands when visiting gentry found themselves compelled to borrow small sums of money from their keepers and beaters. Alice shuddered at the sight; at least, Jonathan had never been a drinking man, but the fact that he needed spirits now was a sign of weakness that brought her too close against reality.

Jonathan put his fingers to the window, but the ice was too thick for him to make a space except by scraping it away with his nails. His fingertips made little indentations which filmed over again as soon as he took them away. Then buffers clanked as Harold Kershaw backed his engine up. Steam rose up from under the running-boards, thick with the smell of axle oil. The heating system creaked and hissed, but did little more than remind them of their frozen toes and ankles.

They pulled past Ashwood Park and Jonathan breathed hard against the pane, rubbed and polished till the glass squeaked under his fingers. But there was nothing to be seen outside. The night was solidly dark. And no man would be fool enough to have any kind of carriage out in the Dale on a night like this. The lights from the carriage windows undulated over the drifts in the valley, the limbs of trees over-burdened on the side of the prevailing north-easterly, the branches sagging with snow and the twigs pendulant with icicles.

They slowed down to a creeping speed and finally came to a halt before the main-line junction at Blackwell Mill.

'We'll never get through,' Alice said.

'They've been getting through all day.'

'They were talking about the points icing up.'

In spite of the blast Jonathan lowered the window. He leaned out to see what was happening. There was nothing he could do about it, but he was a man who had to pit his will-power against the elements.

'It's all right. It's the signal. The express coming through.'

'That's our train. We shall miss it.'

'We shan't.'

A row of lights scudded past them. They saw the roaring glow of an open fire-box thrown back from the hanging smoke.

8

'Going the other way. We're all right.'

They jerked back into motion. Alice closed her eyes and tried to settle her head against the back of the seat. But she opened them wearily again after a few seconds.

'It defeats me,' Jonathan said. 'I never have understood what she ever saw in him.'

'I've told you before. I've told you many times. He was a catch for Miriam Bennett.'

'I've never seen it. I don't see it now. She must have known she'd never change him to her ways.'

'Perhaps she didn't want to. Do people of that age know what it is they do want? Did we? Did *you*?'

He looked at her, his eyes slightly blood-shot from the unaccustomed spirit, full of fear of what she might be going to say next, ready to compensate himself, she knew, with a bout of futile rage.

'I tell you, Jonathan, Jonty was a catch for Miriam Bennett. What had she ever known of decency and love? What had she ever seen of living, before she went to work in that public house? And it wasn't all honey and high living in the *Little Rose*.'

'You're on her side,' Jonathan said.

'I'm not. How can you say such a thing? But I do know what she saw in Jonty—what she thought she saw.'

'She must have known he was never earning enough for her scheme of living.'

'Who ever knows that? When young people are in love, they always think there's going to be enough. Had we enough, do you think? Have we enough now?'

'We've lasted, anyway, you and I.'

'Yes,' she said, dispassionately.

'If I'd only been home at the time.'

'Let's not talk of might-have-beens,' she said.

It was Walter, their second son, who worked in a shop, and therefore heard what people were talking about, who first came home with the news that something was more

9

than awry in the affairs of Jonty and Miriam. But Walter in possession of news was not quite the same thing as Walter imparting it. Walter was a reluctant talker, even when the news he bore might have been welcome. Now he imparted nothing. Only someone who knew him as well as his mother did could have said that he was more than usually uninformative. Walter was worried about something. And she detected that he was skilfully avoiding being alone with her.

Then, one evening, Jonty and Miriam called—not in itself a remarkable event, though visits from either of them had become increasingly rare, and nowadays Jonty more often came alone. But this time they were together, and they could not hide the tension between them. It was evident from her pouting conversation that Miriam was here against her will. She took no interest in what was going on in the house, barely acknowledged Alice's greeting, avoided direct answers to any questions. She could not even be bothered to throw her usual sweetly snide comments in the direction of Edith and Martha, who were sorting wool clippings for rug-making.

At the end of very few minutes, Jonty looked at his watch and said they would have to go. And Miriam demanded a cab—they lived in a cottage up on Burbage Edge, a mile and a half away.

'Cab? We've no need of a cab. It's a lovely evening, and we've all the time in the world.'

'Don't be so mean,' she said. 'In any case, I've money of my own.'

And she swung the little bag, ornamented with rattling glass beads, that she tried to get everyone to call her reticule.

'Well, if you want a cab out of your own money, you can have it. I shall walk.'

Jonty kissed his mother, and Miriam looked round for Walter, to send him down to the rank.

His mother cornered him after they had gone.

'Walter—what's going on between those two? You've heard something, haven't you?'

'It's nothing,' he said.

'Nothing's a big word.'

'They've been having rows. The neighbours have heard them.'

'Rows about what?'

'How should I know? All married couples have rows, don't they?'

'It doesn't sound like Jonty, somehow.'

'Why should Jonty be different from anybody else?'

It was two or three days later that someone in a cabbies' shelter told Jonathan that his son had left the cottage and was living in lodgings at the lower end of the town. He came home and broke the news without tact. But when Alice pressed him for further details, he became embarrassed, reticent and finally angry. She had to turn again to Walter.

'Is nobody going to tell me what's happening to my own first-born?'

'I don't know what's happening to him. I only know what people are saying.'

'And what are people saying?'

'I don't think it's fair to Jonty for me to tell you that.'

'What have I ever refused you, Walter?'

'They say she's been meeting some of her old friends.'

'Where and when was this, then?'

'At the *Little Rose*.'

'She's not gone back there?'

'To help out.'

The situation drove Alice near to the point of illness. She was at an age when she could no longer tolerate the unfamiliar. But she summoned up her energy, put on her Sunday skirts and went to see Jonty at the Town Hall, where he worked as a clerk in the Rating Office. He took her to the privacy of a dusty little store-room, stacked with old ledgers, and found a broken-armed old chair for her to sit on.

And he told her it was true. He had left Miriam. No; he was not paying her anything. She could fend for herself. There was no self-pity about him, no catch in his voice. He might have been talking about yesterday's weather. She saw in him the unreasoning obstinacy of the Bonsalls and something knotted up inside her; the obstinacy of the Bonsalls was limitless and blind. Didn't she know it?

She went home and was sick. She had been sick many times since then. She felt sick again on the train, from the effort of trying to make any kind of explanation to Jonathan. If people's motives were ever at variance with what he imagined his own might have been, then Jonathan never understood. And there were some things that he always did try to turn his back on. Like death, for example. Jonathan Bonsall was more afraid of death and dying than any man she had ever met. When the message had come that his own father was sinking, at the grey stone farm over on Peak Low, he had thought of every excuse to make himself late, had taken the long footpath over the hills and had arrived after the sheet had already been drawn up over the tortured features.

Yet the pair of them had much in common in face of this blow that had been struck at them in their middle-aged simplicity. For they were simple people: their beliefs were simple, their demands were simple, their living was as simple as it was impoverished. And what sprang from roots outside that simplicity was an enigma to them. Alice harboured no illusions about the treatment she had had at the hands of Jonathan—but she had never had a shadow of a doubt about his fidelity. Even when he had thrown up and left her, with nine children in a two-bedroomed cottage, and gone off to South Africa to fight the

Boers, she had never feared that he might turn his eyes towards another woman.

So what Miriam had done to Jonty lay outside the true grasp of their experience.

The brakes squealed for Miller's Dale, the lights of the junction signal-box seeming to skirt their carriage window. The platform was practically deserted: it was a station that had played a great part in their lives—the portal for their annual visits to her old home amidst the brown peat-dykes of the Fens; and for their return again to the green swelling, scree-scattered hills. Harold Kershaw waved to them casually from the foot-plate as he shunted his train out of the path of the oncoming slow from Manchester to Derby. The cold was ruthless. Jonathan unbuttoned his coat and put his flask to his lips again.

'I wouldn't have too much of that, if I were you,' Alice said.

Jonathan looked at her, uncertain whether to become irascible, then tipped the mouth-piece away from his lips and screwed back the silver cap.

'It's a different kind of courage that you and I might need tonight, Jonathan.'

'I wish you wouldn't talk like that.'

'What's the use of talking any other way? What's the use of not being ready for what might be?'

They climbed into another compartment, warmer than the last, but repulsive from the stale breath of crowded passengers. Now they did not talk. They could not sit together, not even opposite each other, separated by the knees of a bearded man asleep and the voluminous skirts of a raw-nosed widow.

Several weeks after they had begun to take his new mode of life for granted, Jonty had come to see them.

'I've come to tell you, so it won't come as a surprise to you, that you'll be seeing my name in the *Advertiser*.'

'Oh? What have you been up to, then?'

He told them that Miriam was playing the pathetically deserted wife and suing him for maintenance.

'Well, all you've got to do is tell them what really happened. She might find herself having to change her boots before she's finished.'

'No point in that,' Jonty said.

'Why not, for goodness' sake?'

'No proof. No witnesses. I've talked to one of the solicitors in the Town Clerk's department. It's all what they'd call hearsay. Nobody will come forward. Nobody wants to get involved, you see.'

Jonathan attempted to release them from the situation with a full-blooded and irrelevant oath.

'But how are you going to afford it?' Alice persisted. 'It'll be like having two homes to keep.'

'It'll not cost me a penny.'

'How do you make that out? They're bound to believe her if you're not going to stand up for yourself and—'

'It'll not cost me a penny for the simple reason that I shall not be paying her a penny. They can carry me out of that court-house in a wooden box before I'll unbelt a farthing for her.'

'Oh, Jonty!'

Monsal Dale—Great Longstone—Hassop—Bakewell—Rowsley—Oil lamps flickered on the snow-bound stations and long shadows fell in irregular triangles over the metal advertising placards: Mazzawattee, Monkey Brand and Bumsted's Royal British Table Salt. When they reached Derby, the snow had started to fall again. It swirled in under the arches of the station, whipped about their legs as they crossed the foot-bridge. And as they emerged into Midland Road, it was lashing the columns of the street lamps, sheeting in front of the brick walls of the warehouses.

Neither of them knew which way to go.

'You'll have to ask,' Alice said. 'You're not going to leave me to do *that*, now are you, Jonathan, *please?*'

So he shouted across to a man in a cap who was pass-ing under the sill of a lighted office window. But most of his words were lost in the blizzard—and there were some things that a man was loth to shout a second time. Jona-than had to cross the road, and stop the man by his elbow, and ask again.

'Can you tell me the way to the—to the prison?'

Jonty had stood like a soldier in the dock, his head only slightly bowed, and that because even at the height of his obstinacy he could not escape his own sense of shame. He told them that he refused to pay even a token of what was demanded. And the magistrate, a not unkindly man, to whom the Bonsalls were not entirely strangers, looked for a moment as if he might try to argue some warm-hearted sense into this well-groomed young man who certainly did not look as if he belonged behind the spiked rail. But evidently he thought better of it, for after a second's delay he scratched something with his pen and rolled his blotter over what he had written.

'Very well, then. You'll go to prison for twenty-eight days. Take him down, please.'

Alice had walked back across the Market Place with her eyes fixed on the trodden snow. Jonathan had blasphem-ously refused to attend the court.

Now it was a police constable who had called, hammer-ing in a manner to bring everyone in the street to their windows. Jonty was dangerously ill in the prison hospital.

'We shall never get through tonight,' Jonathan said. 'If we do, we shall never get back.'

'There is a train. And there's one we can come back on, but we shall have to change at Chinley. I sent Edith down to find out.'

'They'll never let us in at the time of night that we shall get there.'

'Of course they will. Do you think they'd have gone to

15

all this trouble to send for us, if they were going to turn us away again? It's the *hospital* he's in . . .'

'It's all the same. We'd best leave it till the morning.'

'If that's all you think of your son, I shall go on my own. You can leave it till tomorrow morning if you want to.'

'I'll come with you, Mother.'

That was Walter, looking up from a pile of invoices that he had had to bring home from the shop.

'Nay. I'll come.'

They found the gaol, with its cruelly ugly iron-studded gate, and it was a long time after Jonathan had pulled at the bell that a warder came, dangling a key on an enormous ring. He took their names, and seemed not to know their business, and for a long while they were kept waiting in the white-washed office under the gateway arch, with its leather-spined registers and its loudly ticking round-faced clock. At last another man came, solemn, and looking a little like the old Prince Consort. He said that he was the Governor's Assistant, and that he was very sorry, but their son had passed away earlier that evening of pneumonia, which he had contracted before the end of his sentence.

'That'll be from the cold, damp places you've been keeping him in,' Alice said.

They had to follow this man down badly lit, stone flagged passages to the mortuary, and stood looking at Jonty's bloodless, hungry features until the Governor's Assistant, asking with his eyes whether they had seen enough, covered the face and led them back along the corridor.

'I'm very sorry, Mr and Mrs Bonsall. Very sorry indeed. He was attended by the finest doctor in Derby and the nurse did not leave his side throughout the last twelve hours.'

He looked as if there was no more to say. His eyes had not really been on them as he said it. Then he raised them, and looked specially at Alice.

16

'At least, there is one thing, if it can come as a crumb of consolation to you. He had served his sentence. That was behind him—completed, to be precise, at eight o'clock last Friday morning. Within the meaning of the words, you can at least be assured that he did not die during a term of imprisonment.'

Alice and Jonathan struggled through the storm back to Midland Road. For a long time they sat in the draughty waiting-room. The station was deserted of people, yet noisy and dirty with its nightly business: a saddle-tank shunting engine was performing a manoeuvre with three empty wagons that appeared now at this platform, now at that, sometimes in front of the shuttered book-stall, sometimes behind it.

At last a porter pulled open the door, kicking wedges of snow from under his heels.

'Are you waiting for something special, then?'

'The Buxton train.'

'There'll be no Buxton train tonight, old friend.'

'For Chinley, then. We have to change at Chinley.'

'For Chinley neither. The line's blocked with drifts yon side of Ambergate. The Chinley train hasn't come *in* yet. We shan't be seeing it before morning.'

'Somebody might have told us,' Alice said.

'To my mind there'll be nothing going north out of this station much before noon tomorrow at the soonest. If I were you, I'd go round to the Bobby station and see if they can fix you up in one of the cells for the night.'

Jonathan got up slowly from the bench, went up to the porter and seizing him by the coarse black stuff of his uniform jacket punched him first across the mouth and then under one eye, and then, with a back-hand swing across his ear, sent him sprawling across the fender-irons.

CHAPTER TWO

I had no difficulty in piecing together what had happened
in the prison and on Midland Road Station. Railways had
played a memorable part in Jonathan Bonsall's life. He
had been of an age to play truant from his village school
the afternoon they worked the first train up from Blackwell Mill on the new branch-line to Buxton. Many families
made an outing of it, but not Jonathan's father, a dour old
man who kept an ale house and a stony-acred farm
amongst the hills above Peak Forest. Old Bonsall had
fathered his son late in life; he was old enough to have
fought at Waterloo, where the regimental bands had blown
their lungs out to drown the screams of the wounded in
the squares. Never since then had he allowed any man
to inveigle him within ear-shot of any function where
music was being played, whether it be on fair-ground
organ or pavilion bandstand.

It had been on the same afternoon that young Jonathan
had received a present from Mad Mike, the Irish foreman
of one of the gangs of navvies who had driven the line up
the limestone dale. The gift had been an old field cannon
from the Peninsular War which had ended its days signalling meal-breaks up and down the workings. For
months afterwards, the lad had kept it hidden in a disused
lime-kiln, wheeling it in a barrow from hamlet to hamlet
under cover of twilight, firing prodigious charges of powder
pilfered from his father's store. Finally, as a gesture against
humanity when his father had told him he would have
to leave home, he had filled the barrel with cement and
had given it several days to set before kindling a spark
to the fuse. It was a wonder he was not killed. There was

not a window left in Peak Low, and they found bits of twisted metal a quarter of a mile away.

All this I knew. Although Jonathan would sometimes walk at my side for a morning or an afternoon without opening his mouth, there were other days when he felt inclined to talk and it was my turn to be silent.

I knew when they ushered me into his cell in Derby gaol that this afternoon was not going to be one of his talkative ones. If ever a man did not belong in confinement, it was Jonathan Bonsall. They had cropped his hair. The clothes in which they had taken him were creased and threadbare. But it was the injustice of it—as he saw it—that had broken his spirit—that and his own tortuous but unrelenting sense of shame. Officially, he was an innocent on remand until the prosecution had proved their case at his trial. But, I reflected, as he stood up with startled politeness when I entered, his shadow had already fallen on the scaffold. There could not be a warder in the prison, not a clerk in the court, not a juryman in the box who would see any need for the facts that the law would present. Of course, no evidence could be brought about the violence in his character. But, as if a spare accusation were needed, in case Crown counsel fell asleep on his feet, there was another charge on the file that they could still fall back on: an outrageous assault on a railway porter who had only tried to be helpful. But that was likely to remain uncleared on the books after the trap had fallen.

Jonathan Bonsall was fifty-one the afternoon I talked to him in his cell. He had been about fifteen the first time I had met him, and I was ten years older than him. A Sunday morning in Dovedale: the lick of a braided line across the shade of a bottle-green pool. And suddenly I was into a two-pound brown trout with a fly of my own devising.

But I had grown careless. After some hours of failure I

19

had been tempted out on to a water-washed stone quite three yards from the bank below the Nabbs, unpardonably parted from my gear. And I would have lost both my balance and that fish had it not been for the boy who, I knew, had been watching me without word or movement from the bank for the last two hours. I knew that he had been gazing at me, keenly learning. And I had affected not to notice him. It was pleasant and undemanding to be quietly admired by a lad in ambush. The cast of my line was sibilant across sunlight and shadow.

Then suddenly he was nimbly alongside and handing me my net, untroubled by the icy current swirling about his knee-breeches.

We laid the fish in my creel in a nest of grass and dock-leaves and I invited the boy to share my lunch: cold legs of pheasant and a mug of cool ale. We sat with our backs to a hazel-bush and I luxuriated in a flush of talk after my hours of silence.

The boy said hardly anything; just sat and listened with his eyes at once restless and penetrating. I cannot remember all I talked about. Politics—I was just waking to the conviction that the world as we knew it was likely to end in our own life-time. I must have talked a good deal of nonsense, too—fallacious paradoxes and flashy aphorisms. Much of it was above Jonathan Bonsall's head; but this did not matter to either of us. He was impressed for the simple reason that he did not understand. And I must have said some embittered things, too, because then, at twenty-five, I felt that I had a great deal to be bitter about. I remember telling him that man had no more protection against the fickleness of woman than had a wily old trout against the flash in the sunlight of an unfamiliar morsel.

'Well, Jonathan—'

He moved his prison chair for me to sit on, perching himself awkwardly on the edge of his bed-boards.

'I've come to try to organise some sort of defence for you.'

He looked at me with a sudden flash of hope: the first he must have seen for more than a week. And at once I felt obliged to squash it once and for all: it would not do for him to live in hope. I was here because his Alice had appealed to me for my help—a woman whom one could not deny. (She had appealed to me a few weeks previously, to help her son, too, and for him I might perhaps have been able to do something, but he had refused to be represented in court.)

'I seem to remember,' I said, 'that there was a previous occasion when I undertook to stand up for you against all charges.'

He nodded. I didn't know whether he knew what I was talking about or not. That, too, had been many years ago —not very long after our first meeting in the haunts of Walton and Cotton.

I was a guest at a weekend house party up at Corbar Edge Hall: a mansion full of cork-screw antlers, pegged-out tiger skins, weird Indian musical instruments and portraits of Lord Dalhousie. Our host was Brigadier-General Sir Reginald Redbourne-Digby, a nostril-quivering old war-horse who had helped in the tidying-up after the Mutiny. The official record said of one of his charges that, 'Its ultimate success was the only justification for the tactics he adopted.' He must also have been one of the most situation-prone soldiers in the history of the Empire. Within five minutes of the first shot of every one of his major engagements he contrived to sustain some injury which would have sent any other officer on a stretcher back to base; but which Redbourne-Digby carried with him, bleeding, limping, bandaged, arm-in-sling, patch-over-eye until the trumpet's final triumph.

We were drinking in his library after lunch, mostly young soldiers and a handful of diplomats when the Regimental Sergeant-Major (his butler) announced that Mac-Taggart, the head keeper, had apprehended a poacher up in the North Warren.

'March him in, then.'

I had no reason to be thinking of Jonathan Bonsall, and at first I did not recognise the dirty, frightened, crippled youth who was paraded capless in front of the old man's desk.

'Prisoner and escort, left wheel! Mark time! Halt!'

The fire-eating Scot and the arthritic warrant officer stood on either side of the boy.

'Sir, on Sunday 11 October 1876, at thirteen minutes to one of the clock, at Corbar Edge Hall, the boy Bonsall—'

Jonathan was covered in mud. His breeches were torn and his leg had bled badly. I knew what had happened. Although such contraptions had been illegal for some years now, MacTaggart had caught him in a man-trap. There had been poaching on the estate on a scale that called for monumental measures.

'—trespassing in search of conies. Well, boy, answer the General Officer Commanding-in-Chief. What have you to say to this charge?'

From Jonathan's point of view, this was not amusing. Apart from his physical injuries, these were still the times when boys of his age were being sent to prison for crimes no more heinous than swimming in canals.

MacTaggart pulled open the boy's jacket to display the capacious extra pockets sewn in its inside lining. There was a guffaw from someone sitting on the club fender.

Jonathan had very little idea of what was going on. It was plain to see that he was taking all his weight on his good leg. The serrated jaws of that appalling machine had taken the skin from below his knee and it was merely by chance that the tibia was not fractured. Moreover, Mac-Taggart had imprisoned him in a boiler-room whilst the Sergeant-Major was reporting his capture, and there was coal dust in his hair, across his forehead and under the reddened rims of his eyes.

'Do you wish to ask any questions of this witness?'

Jonathan stood staring Redbourne-Digby out.

'Very well. If you accept my summary disposal of your case, I shall order MacTaggart to thrash you soundly, then turn you off the premises, on pain of instant prosecution should you ever attempt to return. The alternative—the equivalent of a District Court Martial—will be to be taken before the Justices of the High Peak Hundred and formally charged. I do not think that their proceedings would take very long—or brook much uncertainty.'

One of the Brigadier-General's regimental guests came in with a suggestion.

'Is this not, Sir Reginald, a local emergency? And need we therefore invoke all the machinery of a D.C.M.? Have we not sufficient seniority of rank here to try him at the Drum-Head?'

This brought a murmur of support. They saw the possibilities of a charade. And it suddenly occurred to me that my one chance of helping my young friend was to get in on the game.

'Is it not customary,' I said, 'for the prisoner to be represented? Has he not the right to a prisoner's friend?'

'Defending officer, we call it,' Redbourne-Digby corrected desultorily. 'You're thinking of the Royal Navy.'

'Well, then, Sir Reginald—let Molyneux be Judge-Advocate. O'Toole can prosecute. And I shall be delighted to place my legal experience...'

'Very well, then. But I hope this is not going to take all afternoon. Bed-down after Sunday luncheon. M.O.'s orders.'

I was allowed to take Jonathan to confer in the gun-room. He was much more interested in the racks of fowling-pieces, the pull-throughs, the ramrods and the oil bottles than in what I had to say to him.

'You're a bit of a young ass, aren't you? If you must

poach rabbits, why do you have to pick on the touchiest old flame-gobbler in the county? Let's have a look at that leg of yours—'

It was very nasty indeed.

'We could try to take that further, if you wish. But I'd advise against it. That crowd will give you about as fair a chance as they would to a checked fox.'

'Yes, Mr Bailey.'

'Leave it to me, then, and just answer my questions yes and no. We'd better not keep them waiting.'

They had set a pyramid of museum-piece drums in front of the library table. There was a good deal of laughter and esoteric irrelevance. He was made to remain standing. At last my turn came.

'You have a Christian name?' I asked him.

'Yes, sir.'

'And what is it?'

'Jonathan, sir. Jonathan Bonsall.'

'You were not by any chance christened *The Boy*?'

Jonathan did not understand what I was getting at. I preferred him not to.

'No, sir.'

I turned to the court.

'I submit, then, that the charge-sheet is wrongly made out. There can therefore be no case to answer, a non-existent person having been accused. I will also ask the prisoner to roll up the leg of his breeches—'

'Wait,' said the one who was playing Judge-Advocate. 'Defending Officer has made a submission upon a point of military law. Court will adjourn for legal argument—'

I did not step outside with Jonathan again. The interest in his immediate future soon petered out. Redbourne-Digby was already nodding off. The presence of the prisoner in an ante-room was soon forgotten. I was the one who had to remind the R.S.M. to dismiss him from the premises.

And, standing where I was in the bow-window of the library, I saw him go: limping round by the corner of the stables, striking out in a diagonal line towards the Warren in which he had been caught. I did not put it past him to collect the remainder of his morning's bag from some cache or other.

But suddenly I saw another figure running across the lawn from a corner of the terrace: a house-maid in brown livery and a white lace cap, with the bows of her apron flying about behind her. She called Jonathan over to her and gave him a small packet done up in brown paper. They talked very briefly, and then she came flying back across the turf, Jonathan hobbling off with a pause every time his left foot touched the ground.

It was his first meeting with Alice Offord. I did not then, of course, know her name, but I had seen her about the Hall: who could have missed those brown compassionate eyes, grave and wondering, yet struggling often to suppress some secret mirth?

It was a long time ago: nine births in cottage bedrooms for Alice Offord—and her eldest son already laid out before her on that slab in the shameful heart of the county town. It was difficult to look at Jonathan, close-cropped and wild in captivity, and remember all that had happened in between.

'Yes,' I said. 'I got you off at the Drum-Head on what we call a technicality. It's going to need a technicality again this time. I can't think that any other kind of defence will do us much good. And I'm afraid we're going to have to hunt on our hands and knees for something that will impress the Assizes.'

'Yes,' Jonathan said. He had an unbounded faith in me, which I found in itself almost heart-breaking.

'In the meanwhile,' I said, 'there are other complications. Quite apart from that bit of play-acting when you stepped on MacTaggart's trap, you had to face a real Court Martial outside Magersfontein, didn't you?'

'I got off,' he said sulkily.

I had never heard the full details, but the case was notorious—with all that wealth of local embroidery that comes from lack of real knowledge.

'I'm not saying that it matters now,' I said. 'Nobody can quote it against you—especially since you were acquitted. But it's bound to influence the way people think. So I want you to tell me about it.'

'It was Stanley Redfern,' he said. 'From my cousin's workshop. We'd joined up together.'

I knew that. Patriotic fervour apart, it was no credit to Jonathan to have left his family. Nor was I convinced that patriotic fervour had played much part at all.

'It got so that Stanley Redfern couldn't stand it—the skirmishes and patrols. He wanted us to shoot each other in the foot—standing quite a way apart, so there wouldn't be any powder-burns. Then we'd be written off as wounded and get sent home. I wasn't having any. They'd never have believed that we both had the same sort of wound, would they? But Stanley went on about it so much that he talked himself into thinking that I'd said I'd come in on it with him. Came one morning, we'd both been on guard the last two hours before sunrise, and I saw him on the edge of the compound, taking aim at my ankle and signalling to me to do the same to him. I could see he really was going to pull the trigger. So I shot him.'

'Dead?'

Jonathan nodded.

'And they believed you?'

'They seemed to. Mind you, they had me in the guard room six weeks.'

'My God, Bonsall. And if some of the tales I've heard are true, the only reason you were in South Africa was because you'd quarrelled with your wife about going to a dance.'

26

'There was more to it than that,' Jonathan said.

'Bonsall—I don't know why I bother with you.'

I did. It was connected with a pair of brown grieving eyes when his Alice had come to see me in my office. Her love for him did not seem to have shrunk at all—even though she must have known his selfishness and lack of self-control as well as she knew the creases at the wrists of her nine babies.

'Oh, Mr Bailey—when you stand up in that court...'

'I shan't be standing up in court, Jonathan. I am a solicitor. Only a barrister can stand up in that court. I shall have to brief counsel for you.'

'Oh,' Jonathan said, confidence implicit.

'And that will cost money. Which you haven't got. But you don't have to worry on that score. For the memory of a trout that I once saw you tickle out of the weeds in the lower reaches of the Lathkill, I'll mark the brief for you. That means I'll pay the fees out of my own pocket. But Jonathan: I've got to know what happened.'

'I didn't kill her, Mr Bailey.'

I had known that I would have to hear the formula sooner or later.

'Tell me what time you got back home from Derby.'

'It was after midday the next day. We stayed all night in that waiting-room. It was cold. I wanted Alice to finish my whisky, but she'd never allowed strong drink to pass her lips. And we could have done what that porter said: we could have asked the Bobbies for a bed. But that's something that neither of us could have faced.'

'I can understand that.'

'So we got home. And I had a rest. Then come the late afternoon, I went down to the *Little Rose*.'

'Having sworn in a dozen public places what you were going to do when you got there?'

'No. Not that. I'd promised Alice I was going to keep my temper. I didn't go there to make trouble. But that Miriam

27

had some of Jonty's bits and pieces that we wanted back. There was a *jardinière*, amongst other things, that had come from Peak Low.'

'But she wasn't working in the inn, was she, so soon?'

'She was upstairs. She'd gone back there to live. Mabel Mosscrop said she didn't think she was well enough to come down, but she'd go up and see.'

'Did you create a fuss?'

'I was quiet, Mr Bailey. There were people in the bar that knew me: Sam Critchlow and two or three gentlemen. They all stopped talking when they saw me come in.'

'I can imagine.'

'I didn't want a drink. I needed a plug of twist, but I meant to wait and go elsewhere for it. There was none of my money going over the counter of the *Little Rose*. I went out across the yard, not because I really wanted to, but to give me somewhere to go, something to do, while Mabel Mosscrop was seeing Miriam. I couldn't stand there with those gentlemen's eyes fixed on me. And Sam Critchlow. You perhaps wouldn't understand, Mr Bailey.'

Why do people always seem to think that my style of life is so removed from theirs that I can never have experienced a human emotion at first hand?

'You went into the yard—?'

'And she was lying on the cobbles, dead, Mr Bailey. I've seen sights in my time, and I never want to see one like that again.'

'And it had been done with your own axe?'

'Jonty had borrowed it—oh, weeks before that. He'd no right to have taken it without telling me. And Alice had no right to let it go out of the house without asking me first.'

'All right, Jonathan. Let's stick to the subject. You picked it up?'

'It was mine, wasn't it? And God knows what else it had been used for. The state of its edge...'

28

'Jonathan: if you go into the witness-box and tell the jury that your one reaction in this situation was that some-one had ruined the temper of your axe...'

'I can't explain it properly, Mr Bonsall. It's funny what ideas come into your head at all the wrong moments.'

'All the same: I'd keep quiet about that one if I were you. You picked up the axe. And Mabel Mosscrop came out into the yard...'

'Screaming at the top of her voice.'

He had folded his prison blankets in the fashion of army kit at the head of his bed. I did not know whether that was prison discipline or a relic of his military training. It was not easy, looking at him in that cell, to think of the boy, the youth that I had known. For all his crass stupidity in some of the situations I had seen him in, I had to confess a liking for Jonathan Bonsall. Once, not long after I had first got to know him, I had suggested to him that he might become my regular ghillie at weekends and on holidays. But he had simply avoided giving me any answer. He came out with me many times after that, but never as part of any formal agreement. And I never again pressed him on the point. He was a man born and shaped for freedom.

'Tell me,' I said. 'They went for Constable Gill. Can you remember what was the first thing you said to him, when he told you he was going to take you to the lock-up? This is important, Jonathan.'

'Only that I hadn't done it.'

'And you went for him with the axe, I suppose?'

By his answer I knew that we were down to honesty in its simplest form.

'I may have looked as if I were going to.'

'And you can look me in the eye and assure me that you hadn't killed her?'

'I'm not a killer, Mr Bailey.'

'You killed Stanley Redfern.'

'I didn't want my foot shot off, did I?'

'And you're lucky you didn't kill that railway porter. If he'd fractured his skull against the hearth-stone . . .'

'I wouldn't hit a woman, Mr Bailey.'

'So who do you think did?'

'How am I to tell? She was already dead.'

'So tell me who were those gentlemen in the bar when you walked in.'

'There was Sam Critchlow.'

'Yes. I know. He usually drops in on his way to and from his work. A personal friend of the house, you might say. And the others?'

'I don't know all their names. They weren't all Buxton men. There was that old chap who comes up sometimes from Leicester.'

'Mr Weigall.'

'And one or two others. I didn't take all that much notice of them. I was wishing they weren't there. I didn't want anyone to see me, let alone talk. I've told you: that's why I went out across the yard.'

I took my leave of him shortly after that, trying not to feed his confidence falsely, yet hard put to it not to drop him a crumb or two of hope. It was the least I could do, as I left him to the routine of cracked bells and rattling keys and clanking doors: and warders who were already speculating which pair of them would be standing at his elbow at the side of the drop.

Why did I occupy myself with such a hopeless issue? Was it because I thought—could any man possibly think? —that he was telling the truth? Was I sentimental fool enough to think that Jonathan Bonsall could not tell me a lie?

Or was it because I, too, hated Miriam Bennett for what she had done to a family who had played a large part in the not inconsiderable margins of my life? Was she likely to take yet another of them with her down her chute to hell, oiled with cheap scent and ambergris?

Did I for a moment believe that Jonathan Bonsall had not swung that axe? Did I believe that even if he hadn't, there was some slender chance of ever proving it?

I went into the *Little Rose* directly I stepped off the train that brought me back from Derby. I was no stranger to the inn. It was a house that catered almost as intimately as a family circle for a certain type of man, of whom I am one, in the years of Buxton's late Victorian and Edwardian zenith. I had known Miriam Bennett even before Jonty Bonsall had met her—but only from a distance: that remoteness of observation, speculation and fantasy that can save a man from the sort of trouble that Jonty laid up for himself.

Almost always when I had been away from Buxton, even for a mere afternoon, the first twenty minutes after my return were passed in the *Little Rose*. After that, I felt I was back in the bosom of the town.

Perhaps it would be useful to say a word about the town of Buxton—the Spa of Blue Waters—in the first decade of this century. Those same curative springs had been known to the Romans, but it had taken the advent of the railway, whose first train Jonathan Bonsall had watched from a lip of overhanging rock, to bring in the hydropathic swarms. The sciatic, the rheumatic, the gouty, the arthritic and the frankly senile could further penalise their digestion at the starched linen of its tables, could bathe in its azure waters and sip the tepid draughts of St Anne's Pump Room. They could shop under its colonnades, read romances from its circulating libraries, be drawn in glass-fronted bath-chairs along its tree shaded promenades. There was a glass-domed ballroom and a concert hall with palms. There was an Opera House with twin cupolas, a broad staircase and a proscenium curtain after Fragonard. There were churches high and low, chapels strict and evangelical. The more venturesome could ride in coaches and wagonettes through the green dales and spine-chilling gorges of the limestone hills.

The general run of visitors were well enough catered for to have no need of the special atmosphere which the *Little Rose* provided. For the most part the infirm and the over-sheltered had neither call nor temptation to cross its threshold. There was an ambience about the *Little Rose* that was not even noticed by those who would not have appreciated it.

Those of us who did came from no particular professional or social class. We numbered amongst us hopeful god-children attending stooping widows in the town's exclusive convalescent homes; and liver-hobnailed ornaments of for-gotten general staffs. And in addition there descended the occasional exploring tourist who found the Spa's normal pace of revelry disappointing—until he happened on the *Little Rose*. And there were a few who were indigenous Buxtonians: such as Sam Critchlow.

We were all modest drinkers; we were not noisy; the house was no den of immorality. If that had been the case, I would certainly not have been one of its habitués. But if immorality happened to be the panacea for any habitué's discontent—and if he could attain his ends in the *Little Rose*, then that was his affair. But he had to achieve it without bringing any opprobrium to bear upon either the management or the circle of regular guests. We knew how to be discreet in the *Little Rose*—on both sides of the bar counter. The house was not particularly sophisticated, though its fittings belonged to the age that we were living in. But in a rather formalised way—for the twentieth century had only just dawned—it was relaxed. And it was over this hive of disciplined relaxation that Mabel Moss-crop had groomed Miriam Bennett to preside.

Situated as it was, with an unobtrusively narrow frontage on the Quadrant, the *Little Rose* was well placed for its complex role. It was tucked away in the very heart of the town, yet did not encroach upon the town's more formal Establishment. For the parched palates and stiffened limbs of those who had just journeyed up by Midland Railway, it was a natural first call. A stone thrown from the Hospital or the Thermal Baths could have broken one of its windows. It was two minutes' walk from the Opera, the Pavilion and the shops of Spring Gardens. If one crossed the road to the General Post Office, one had only to mistake a door to walk into one of Miriam Bennett's entrail-twisting smiles.

I knew, of course, a little about Miriam. I knew that Mabel Mosscrop's discovery of her potential had been at once a stroke of genius and a partial accident. For her first few years at the *Little Rose* she was just another girl who had left school at twelve, but who looked as if she never ailed physically and would therefore not be forever taking time off for sickness, and whose family badly needed (and knew how to squander) the shillings that she earned. And if the drudgery was back-breaking, the hours long, the quarters bare and the winters dark and cold, these were not hardships with which to impugn Mabel Mosscrop's sense of humanity. One might as justly have arraigned her for employing a twelve-year-old in an era in which every twelve-year-old of her acquaintance was employed. It is in the nature of winters—especially of winters in the High Peak of Derbyshire—to be long, dark and cold, and it was in the nature of work behind the scenes in an Edwardian inn to be hard, for hours to be long, holidays and outings rare and wages meagre.

And Mabel Mosscrop was not unkind. She could be tart, but she was not vicious; she was sometimes angry, but without being hurtful, exasperated but not vindictive. If she sometimes seemed to drive her servants like slaves, she herself worked as hard as any two of them together. She was always ready to leap forward and help a child to turn

33

a bed that was too heavy for her. She was quite likely to empty the chamber-pots herself and leave the girl to fetch fresh water for the ewer. Amongst work to be done, she did not recognise any social hierarchy. Nor would she waste spoken pity on arms scalded red by constant immersion in hot water; but she was ready at the end of the day to offer her own bottle of calamine lotion, or a block of Melrose for rubbing into chapped hands. She could work like an Irish navvy, be incubating a cold into the bargain and still attend to her customers with composure. And at the same time she appeared to keep her habitually drunken husband placidly managed, too.

All this I knew—but without involvement. I am not a writer—I am far too lazy—but I like to think that I can enjoy the writer's state of constant observation in depth without, in the normal run of life, the fatigue of having to put any of it down. From my quiet corner in the *Little Rose*—and along its gloomy corridors, when, as occasionally happened during domestic upheavals, I have stayed in the hotel for a few nights—I have been watching Mabel Mosscrop and Miriam Bennett for years.

But I knew that if there did exist a narrow loop-hole through which I might possibly prise some help for Jonathan Bonsall, then there was a good deal of supposition that I had to turn into established fact. An idle writer gets out of the habit of discipline; he does not have to weave his fantasies to suit anyone's preferences but his own. It is true that I am a lawyer, too; but also a lazy one.

Was it just another self-delusion, that Jonathan Bonsall might ever fill his lungs with open air again?

I did not propose to cross-examine anyone in the *Little Rose*; but I knew that I was going to have to persist with one or two questions that could make me very unpopular.

CHAPTER THREE

'You've been to see him?'

Mabel Mosscrop was appalled at the idea. It was tantamount to mutinous disloyalty to Miriam. Mabel Mosscrop was not exactly wearing mourning—that would have been no way to manage the *Little Rose*—but there was a great deal of black about her costume. She was showing her respect; and yet, in a way, she was subduing her true grief. Miriam had meant a lot to Mabel—and to the Rose.

'You're not going to defend him, are you, Mr Bailey?'

'In English law, a man has the right...'

She shrugged her shoulders; or, rather, they twitched involuntarily. It was the nearest she had ever come, in conversation with me, to showing a personal reaction.

'I'm sure, Mr Bailey, that you would not do anything that you did not think was proper.'

Colder praise never came from woman's tongue. Without having to ask my needs, she prepared my drink: Madeira in water, with the juice of a lime and a pinch of grated nutmeg.

'But if you had heard him say what I heard him say—'

'Yes, Mrs Mosscrop?'

'If it had been you or I who had found a body in a courtyard—Mr Bailey, when I went out there, he was standing with the chopper in his hand, complaining because somebody had taken the edge off it.'

'I know,' I said. 'Disgusting. But...'

'If you can see any *Buts* in that, Mr Bailey, you could see *Buts* in anything.'

It was the nearest I had ever seen Mabel Mosscrop come

35

to forgetting her station. It was one of the comforts of the *Little Rose* that such questions never arose.

'I was going to say, Mrs Mosscrop, that it seems hardly the remark of a man who has just committed murder.'

I had hoped that her intelligence would have enabled her to follow me in this thought, but she looked at me without understanding, and I did not feel equal to the process of explaining myself. Help, however, came to me from the darker corner of the counter.

'I think I know what Mr Bailey means.'

Sam Critchlow was a foreman-shunter who worked unpredictable shift hours in the railway goods-yard. Standing fully six feet six, he was so proportioned that one did not notice him for his height alone. He had served for years in the Royal Navy, but had never been known to tell a story from that part of his life. Yet he always seemed to cultivate a maritime appearance, the upper half of his body always enveloped in an immense blue guernsey.

'I've known Jonathan Bonsall since both of us were lads. I don't like the man but I can't see him killing a woman. Not wilfully, that is.'

'If you'd seen him standing there, with the chopper in his hand—his own chopper...'

'I don't doubt it was his own chopper. But he hadn't brought it with him that afternoon, that's for certain. I was standing here when he walked through and into the yard.'

Mabel Mosscrop heard this without enthusiasm. But factually, she could not deny it.

'And whatever reason Jonathan Bonsall might have had for hating Miriam...'

'And why, if you please, should anybody have hated her?'

This was the line of thought that Mabel Mosscrop badly needed. She looked as if she were going to get her teeth into it.

'I'm not pointing to whose fault anything was,' Sam Critchlow said reasonably. 'I'm stating truths, that's all. Miriam Bennett should never have married Jonty Bonsall. And that's not saying anything about either of them that a man ought not to say. I said it to their faces, too. Both of them.'

'He did,' Mabel Mosscrop said, for my benefit, as if she had some obscure reason for thinking that Critchlow needed her support. As if, too, she was relieved to be able to say something which she knew I might applaud.

Sam Critchlow was a strange man. There were legendary tales of his attitude to women—rumbustious and insatiable. And yet, often as they were told—in his presence as well as behind his back—not one of us could have pointed to any women we could have said for certain he had ever been with. It was believed that he and Mabel were both waiting for Jack Mosscrop to drink himself into the grave; but if this was true, they always kept a very proper distance in public. And he had always been openly and demonstratively fond of Miriam, though on a strictly avuncular plane.

'Who else was in here the afternoon Jonathan Bonsall walked through?'

'Weigall, the commercial traveller, from Leicester. And the man who writes history books.'

'Had either of them—or you yourself—been out across the yard?'

'I hadn't. I can't speak for them. I'd not been in here five minutes myself.'

'The police inspector has been here going over all this,' Mabel Mosscrop said, as if she had resented going through this range of questions even once.

'Which police inspector, Mrs Mosscrop?'

'Inspector Brunt.'

I had heard of him. He was not a man who would take kindly to sharing confidences outside the force. Mabel

Mosscrop took refuge in philosophical comforts.

'Whatever questions any of you ask, they're not going to bring her back.'

'That's true.'

'I feel it badly, you know, Mr Bailey. I was the one who brought her here. I gave her the first job she had after she left school. I watched her grow up. I was like a mother to her.'

This was unanswerable, because it was true. Miriam's own parents lived in a slum cottage amongst a slum settlement that served one of the lime quarries.

'I brought her here. I taught her to hold a knife and fork. I taught her to undress before she went to bed. Funnily enough, she was a lazy child, when she first came here.'

'I know what you mean, Mabel,' Sam Critchlow said. 'Yet lazy's not a word you'd think to use alongside Miriam's name.'

'She was, though. Many's the tray of tumblers I've given her back to polish again. She couldn't see with her own eyes that an ash-tray needed emptying—she'd walk past it a dozen times a day. The same with an empty coal scuttle or a fire that needed making up.'

She began to warm to her reminiscences and I encouraged her. The relief from tension was perceptible.

'And I can remember to the day, almost to the hour, the time she started to grow up. Do you remember Ivy Lake?'

The question startled me. It sounded as if she expected me to know half the women visitors to Buxton.

'She was an actress. Used to play at the Opera House. Not big parts, as a rule, though now and then they'd give her something with a speech or two she had to learn. She always stayed here for the season. Always had Number Five. You *must* have seen her, Mr Bailey—big, well-built woman, not quite so young as she used to be, with a nose like an eagle's.'

In a more playful mood I might have chopped logic

38

over the statement that if a woman had an aquiline nose, I must know her. I might even have expostulated that eagles don't have noses. But I let Mabel Mosscrop continue.

'The thing is, you had to see her dressing-table to believe it—up in her bedroom, I mean. I'm not talking about the stuff she had over at the theatre. Pots, jars and phials. There wasn't a cream, paint or powder on the market that she didn't try the moment it came out. The room looked like a chemist's shop. And, I must say, it smelt like one. She spent two or three hours a day in front of her mirror.'

It was a relief to have Mabel Mosscrop story-telling again.

'I'd reminded Miriam to go up and draw Miss Lake's curtains, turn down the bedcovers and put the hot water bottle in. I can remember to this day the play they were doing that week. It was *The Gay Lord Quex* and she couldn't leave the stage till after the final curtain. Well, I thought Miriam was taking her time, and I went up to see. And there she was. She'd taken out three of Miss Lake's frocks and was trying them on one at a time. When I walked in, she was wearing an American afternoon dress, checked blue, with blue skirts drawn in tight to a high waist. Of course, it was too big for Miriam, but she and Miss Lake were pretty much of a height, and she'd managed to put in a pin or two at the back, so you got an idea of how she might look from in front.'

She interrupted herself to recharge Sam Critchlow's tankard. The wheels of a brougham seethed over the stones of the Quadrant, a creak in the dry axle.

'Then she'd had a go at some of the pots and jars; put rouge over her cheek bones. When I turned the door handle, she was just shaping a Cupid's bow over her lips. "My God!" I said. I couldn't help myself. Miriam started back, thinking I was Miss Lake, come home early for some reason. When she saw it was me, she was even more scared.

And, of course, I ought to have torn her limb from limb. If anything is sacred in a hotel, it is a guest's belongings. But, I say, I couldn't help myself. I just put my hand on her shoulder, turned her round, made a better job of the pins. Then I made her wipe her face clean. Then I had a go at it myself: a touch of eyebrow pencil, a dab of *La Dorine* powder, a spot of Bertrand's *Patchouli* behind the ears. I stood back and looked at her. Then I made her clean herself up, get a dustpan and sweep the powder off the floor, go down and help Jack put a new barrel of four ale on. Which, as we all know very well, meant doing it herself, though Jack might grunt a word or two of encouragement now and then.'

Mabel Mosscrop was under no illusions about her husband.

'I didn't say anything for the next few weeks. I was thinking things out. I had a picture in my mind. I can't describe to you how she'd looked. But perhaps you can imagine. I had the beginnings of an idea. I didn't dream it would ever work as well as it did—but if only she could be made to look as I knew she could look—and then made to live up to it. Two or three weeks later I threw her a couple of my old dresses and told her to make what she could of them. She could be fairly handy with a needle, when she was in the mood for it—which means when she was doing something for herself.'

She said this without malice: a pure statement of fact and observation.

'I put her behind the bar once or twice, for an hour or two. She'd be about seventeen at the time; she had a lot to learn. How to take a little chaff from customers without allowing herself to become too familiar. Yet how to remain in charge without becoming waspish. How to say no to an offer of a drink from a customer. How to accept one—and not drink it. It wasn't easy. I won't say that any of the gentlemen tried it on with her—not any of our regulars, anyway. But she came in for a bit of teasing; and she had to learn to look as if she was enjoying it, without letting it go too far—even when she was tired. It wasn't easy. I had to keep on at her. I think we both came to hate washing-up time, when the king-bolts had been shot. It was always the time for our nightly reckoning. "You still seem to think I'm just a kid," she said once. And I said, "Yes—and I shall go on thinking so until you start showing a bit of grown-up sense." '

'She'd reason to be grateful to you, Mabel.'

'She had, Sam, and later on, I think she did begin to see it that way. One afternoon I took her with me on the train to Manchester. I'd decided that the time had come to give her a bit more responsibility. So I wanted to take her to my own hairdresser, let her choose a couple of dresses of her own—under my eye—bought her a piece or two of costume jewellery. You men would have been the first to notice if she'd stood behind the bar wearing my cast-offs.'

Mabel Mosscrop sometimes had a mind as sharp as a kitten's teeth.

'We had buttered scones in a tea shop in Albert Square —and then I took her into the *Queen's*: a palace, of course, compared with the *Little Rose*. I showed her how a pair of ladies might comport themselves when a head porter in black tie and tails was uneasy at their presence.'

Mrs Mosscrop was an excellent mimic—especially when she had a story in mid-stream, and was not trying very hard. She produced a perfect imitation of an aristocratic tone produced from the palate of a promoted menial.

' "Madame is waiting for someone?"

' "Madame is waiting for two small ports."

'He coughed.

' "I am extremely sorry, Madame—it is a rule of the house—"

'I stood my ground.

41

' "If Madame would perhaps care to wait in the Residents' drawing-room, I could have coffee served—"

' "The very cheek of the man," Miriam said.

'Then I had to tell her that he was only doing his job—as I expected her to do hers. And that there are two ways of treating people. And on our way out, I stopped so that we could look through the doorway of the main bar. I wanted her to see the woman who was queening it over all that mahogany and that expanse of carpet. A woman older than Miriam, it's true—but younger than me. Very white hands, very slender fingers, tapering down from leg-of-mutton sleeves. And a mauve dress—that she could have worn to a concert at the Pavilion. Miriam understood. Both of you saw the progress that she made after that.'

I certainly did. I cannot say that I had been closely aware of the child's development from the back stairs. But I certainly had no difficulty in remembering her at her zenith, when she was presiding over our masculine stronghold: a queen in her own right, with the most expensive coiffure in the town (for which, it now occurred to me, Mabel Mosscrop must always have paid). She was a stringent disciplinarian—commanding others because she was in command of herself; she knew this man's taste in out-of-the-way cigars, and that one's palate for a rare sherry. And she knew how to behave as if she applauded such fine judgement. She knew how to flatter a man without even speaking to him. And I was not one of those who lost sleep or friendship over the subtlety of her favours, but I will admit that I sometimes took an extra schooner that might have remained in the cask if she had not been in my line of vision.

'Aye,' Sam Critchlow said. 'We know where she went from there.'

His own relationship with her had always had a quality of its own. Perhaps he was the one customer in the Rose who could have said anything he liked to her, and got away with it. If Mabel Mosscrop ever spoke to her critically, even with the greatest justification, her first reaction might be a sharp rejoinder, or even half-an-hour of the sulks. But we had the impression that if ever Sam Critchlow spoke to her in serious vein—as he did sometimes, inaudibly to us, at his own corner of the counter— she had to listen equally seriously. His manner with her was both distant and yet close; he never attempted to vie with the young gentlemen who were after flirting with her, though he never missed a nuance or trick of their intentions and machinations. Not once did Miriam show any resentment at anything he said to her; though once or twice she pouted at him behind his back for the benefit of the rest of us.

'Aye. And if it was Jonathan Bonsall that did it, I'd like to be within hearing of the trap when they spring it.'

Mabel Mosscrop shuddered at the phrase. It was only partially, I think, because she thought we expected it of her.

'But if so be old Jonathan had nothing to do with it, then I wish you more strength to your arm, Mr Bailey. And if I remember anything that's gone out of my mind for the moment, then I shall not rest till I've told you.'

I looked towards Mabel Mosscrop, hoping to see her persuaded by the same healthy sentiment. Sooner or later I would have to get down to some detailed considerations about that fatal afternoon, and I was not able to go far without her committed co-operation.

'I shall be glad when we've finished with all this,' she said.

I emptied my glass. I knew we'd barely started yet.

43

CHAPTER FOUR

There were three people I now had to see: Alice Bonsall, Police Inspector Brunt and Jonathan's cousin, Joshua Mycock. It was out of sheer moral cowardice that I went to see the last-named first.

Mycock's headquarters was a workshop and yard in the amorphous grid of streets behind the Market Place. It was to his cousin that Jonathan had been apprenticed when his father had first turned him out of the house: a complicated story. What I wanted to find out was whether Mycock had seen anything of his cousin between his return from Derby and his visit to the *Little Rose*. It might provide a valuable guide to the state of mind that Jonathan was in.

Joshua Mycock was briskly pleased to see me. It was because I had befriended Jonathan as a boy that Mycock had started bringing his business to me: conveyancing, mostly, on land that he was buying up for speculative building. Joshua had come a long way since Jonathan had first been brought to his workshop.

One of the things that I liked about Joshua Mycock was his refreshing bluntness about things. I had, in the prime of my friendship with Jonathan, achieved a sort of working equality with the lad. There were—I hate the conception, but we have to accept it as a fact of life— certain unnatural differences between us. I had been uneasy at first, in case this difference might have embarrassed or inhibited him. I was, after all, as far as he was concerned, a member of the *gentry*. But *gentry* was not an emotive term, as far as Jonathan was concerned. They were simply something that existed. Just as there were ash plantations on Grin Low, so there were retired Surgeon-Admirals living in the expensive *pensions* along the Broad Walk. Once, when the boy was twanging a peeled hazel-stick against the iron railings of the Pavilion Gardens, a purple-faced Duke in a deer-stalker had called to him to stop his disgusting noise. I had watched the incident from a discreet distance. Jonathan had obeyed with startling alacrity, half inclined his head as if in apology; and then, just as the gouty old aristocrat was nodding to himself his satisfaction with the state of the world at large, Jonathan twitched his stick with a supple wrist and ran up a fresh tattoo. It was not a social gesture; it was certainly not a political one; it was purely personal.

Joshua Mycock, however, had arrived at a different— and thoroughly realistic attitude, which he never troubled to put into words. The expansion of the town that had followed the coming of the railway up the Dale had brought untold sovereigns into Joshua Mycock's coffers. Although he had never allowed it to alter his style of life, he was better off by far than most of the gentlefolk who were raising mortgages to buy the houses that Joshua was building. Sometimes it was Joshua himself who lent them their funds. And he talked to all men alike.

He was not impressed by the nature of my inquiry.

'In short, no. I didn't set eyes on Jonathan during the period you mention. I was anxious to know how Alice had taken the blow. But I waited till my spies had told me Jonathan had gone out before I called.'

'You'd lost patience with him?'

'I lost that thirty-five years ago. No; this time I couldn't have guaranteed myself, if he'd come out with something stupid. He always had a touch of violent temperament, Mr Bailey, and yet I'd maintain that there isn't a trace of vice in him. Even if I knew for a fact that he did kill that worthless bitch that ruined his son, I'd still say he was without vice. But he's a man who's always had to fight.

He got into a fight that first afternoon he put his knees under my apprentices' table.'

'I know. He told me about that.'

'It was partly because he was such a glutton that his father threw him out. And partly because his father was a twisted man who didn't know how to treat either his neighbour or himself. When he came to leave school, the boy found himself working for both his father and his uncle, with the run of both their farms. And he knew how to play off one against the other—especially when it came to food. God, he had an appetite, though he never had flesh on his bones to show for it. I don't know where it all went to, but Christ, he could put it away. That last day, the day his father said there was nothing more for him at Peak Low, he was supposed to have mended a wall. He could have been a champion dry-stone waller at the Trials, could Jonathan, if he'd put his mind to it. But when William Bonsall rode down Blackdale Brow that afternoon, he found the lad asleep in the sunshine, and not a stroke of the work done. Mind you, it would have been, if only they'd left him to it. I know Jonathan well enough for that. He'd have done it. But he'd have set about it in his own time. But what upset William Bonsall and his brother was what they found the lad had taken out with him to eat. He was doubling up on his meals already, pleading hungry at one farm, after he'd just eaten at the other. He'd half a cold rabbit pie with him under the shelter of that wall, two pounds of Cheshire cheese, a loaf and a half of bread.'

Joshua Mycock kicked an off-cut of deal under one of the benches.

'They said he'd have to leave home. He was nothing but an extra mouth to feed and he didn't want farm work, anyway. They said he had to serve his time with me as a carpenter—and he didn't want that, either. More's the pity. A finer craftsman I never had through my hands, as

God's my judge, and when he was all but a week out of his time, I offered him a partnership. He could have had his name on the board: Mycock and Bonsall. I showed him how I'd got the new lettering all drawn out ready. But no. He said he was going to be a gamekeeper. "And who the bloody hell's going to take you for a gamekeeper?" I asked him. If there'd been full-time work for a poacher, I'd have put my money on him.

'But he got into a fight, that first night in the workshop. Christ, it was a bloody good scrap, that was. Of course, I didn't have to know anything about it, or I'd have had to stop it. All I could do was watch it through a knot-hole in a shed door. And all over a slice of bread and butter. And, of course, it had to be Stanley Redfern's. He was a year and a half older than Jonathan, longer in the reach. Knew what he was about. He watched young Jonathan take his bread and butter and said nothing till they'd finished their tea. Then he tapped Jonathan on the shoulder and the other lads were already clearing a space in the yard.

'Jonathan could fight. If he went into any village where he wasn't known, you could have said there'd be a bloody nose or two, within ten minutes. And he lashed out at Stanley: great, swinging hay-makers. They'd have laid him flat, if they'd contacted; but Stanley didn't let them contact. They fought, those two, till they were both practically too weak to stay on their feet. But Stanley had saved enough strength for one last swipe: a crack across the jaw that would have split a limestone crag.

'"That'll cost you a ha'penny loaf, young master," Stanley said. "You'll find a baker's shop open in Market Street."

'Only Jonathan hadn't got a ha'penny. All he had was the single gold sovereign his father had given him at their parting. And I happened to know that Jonathan didn't rest till he'd turned his small change back into a

47

gold piece. I'll bet he still had a sovereign in his waist-coat pocket when they stripped him down at Derby gaol. Not quite the same one, but a sovereign, all the same: the sentimental fool.

'That was always more than half the trouble with Jonathan, of course—sentimentality. Only it sometimes found itself a funny way out. Stanley Redfern? They were the best of friends for years. Oh, yes—I know Jonathan shot the silly bugger. So would I have shot him, if I'd seen he was going to put a ball into my bloody foot.

'Poaching? I never saw the bloody like of it. In a way, I always thought I was partly to blame, because when I saw the turn things were taking, I told him on the quiet I could market the odd hare for him. Christ, he'd have had me in business doing nothing else, if I hadn't put an end to it.

'Yet in another way, though, Mr Bailey, it was you who set him off on the wrong foot there, after a manner of speaking.'

I looked at him curiously.

'That night you gave him a couple of tickets to the concert in the Pavilion.'

I laughed. I had to. It was an evening that is still talked about by Buxton's concert-going public.

One Sunday, in Beresford Dale, in the pool by the little stone pavilion that is still called Walton's Temple, I had asked the boy if he liked music. There was a sudden spark of enthusiasm in his eyes; but I discovered to my disappointment that he was thinking of the sort of ballad he had heard about his village. I promised him two tickets for the Pavilion; and I also told him—it was the sort of talk I indulged in far too much, those days—that a man was not musically mature until he had come to appreciate Beethoven's Concerto in C Minor.

I heard from several acquaintances in the audience what happened.

48

The society of the Pavilion, of course, was one in which Jonathan would not normally have thought of moving. It was in particular anathema to Stanley Redfern, who thought of himself as a political firebrand. To him, the Pavilion was a stronghold of wealth and idleness, an esoteric cult for those whose unearned income had discovered yet another way of demonstrating their exclusiveness.

The pair of them dressed for the occasion: their oldest clothes; caps with the lining peeping through the cloth; buttonless old shirts; their working boots laboriously caked with stable dung. They even had the subtlety to arrive a few minutes late.

I had done them proud. Their seats were near the front, and in one of the more expensive rows, so that men had to rise to let them pass, and ladies draw in their knees. The lady on Jonathan's left withdrew like a snail into the furthest corner of her seat, not only in futile self-defence against the filth of his clothes and the smell of his boots, but also against the hazards of his elbows, for Jonathan—who had never seen an orchestral conductor before—was quick to enter into competition with him.

They applauded energetically at the end of the overture, and then there came on to the platform a big-bosomed soprano who was to sing a Schumann song-cycle. To Jonathan it must have seemed the apotheosis of the absurd, with a pianist who sat gingerly on his stool and flicked fastidiously at the keyboard. And the bodisome, big-throated warblings made him stick the end of his little finger in his ear in pursuit of fugitive wax. They clapped vigorously at the end of the first song, which clearly they should not have done, since no one else did, and sat looking shame-faced while the singer waited for the next prelude. Paradoxically, though they were stretching the limits of their imagination to offend against convention, they did not like exhibiting involuntary ignorance.

They had already done enough to throw Madame off

49

her aplomb. She was too disciplined to falter, but there was an extra feverish twist in her handkerchief and she became unable, to the point of mesmerism, to take her eyes off the two dirty hobbledehoys, whom she took to be paid *claqueurs*. She left the stage with tears in her eyes.

The next offering was a suite of Mozart minuets. The timpanist, a bald-headed little stoat of a man with an array of snares, glockenspiels and chime-bars, was either so tactless or genuinely mischievous that he actually winked at Jonathan. And Jonathan, finding the rhythms of the eighteenth century within his compass, began to beat time not only with his hands and arms but with legs and feet as well, so that the whole row of seats was soon creaking in six-eight time.

Jonathan acknowledged the timpanist's wink and pointed to the cellist who, in a bout of sudden activity, was sawing across all four strings in a passage of semi-quaver arpeggios. The timpanist affected not to see him, so Jonathan had to rise from his seat to draw attention to what was obviously the most successful comic turn to date.

'Sit down!' came gruffly from behind. The timpanist, his eye now anxiously following the score, touched a triangle.

'Ping!' said Jonathan. And 'Shut up!' said even Stanley Redfern.

The lady at Jonathan's side was holding her handkerchief to her nose against the composite stench of corduroy, farmyard droppings and old clothes rancid with a decade of labourers' sweat. For some reason or other, she let this handkerchief slip and Jonathan, swooping to retrieve it for her, not only struck her knee with his elbow but unintentionally brought up the hem of her skirt, together with a handful of unmentionably filthy straw. She screamed; and her escort reached over and pushed Jonathan back into his seat, giving his ear a vicious tweak into the bargain.

Jonathan yelped. The conductor looked down backwards over his shoulder. The timpanist turned away to tune a drum.

That was as near as Jonathan ever came in his life to hearing the Third Piano Concerto. He and Stanley Redfern were forcibly ejected at the beginning of the interval, though not much force was needed. They must have realised that the Establishment had everything on its side.

'Aye!' Joshua Mycock said, 'and they walked back through the Gardens in the dark. Uprooted a bed of asters and took two mallards from the ornamental lake; which my wife Naomi found on the larder slab next morning. That's how I came to drop a hint that if ever the odd head of game should happen into his hands—'

'It wasn't fair to the game,' I said. 'I never saw Jonathan's equal at reading a patch of country. That was why I used to like to have him with me.'

He had a knowledge of the wild life of the Peak that extended down to individual creatures. A smallholder knew that a fox was raiding his hen-run; but Jonathan knew which vixen it was, and from which old quarry on Edgemoor. We showed each other the prints of her pads across the powdery snow of a frozen dew-pond. And we knew from a handful of feathers dropped from the side of her jaw where she had paused at a strange scent. He could spot the mark of a hare's rump in the long grasses of a ten-acre field and could identify himself almost to the minute with the animal's movements. He knew where a dog-otter had prowled for a week by a pool on the upper Manifold, before moving off across Ecton Hill towards the Dove in Wolfscote Dale.

'He was the same with a piece of wood,' Joshua Mycock said. 'If there can be genius in carpentry, then Jonathan Bonsall was a genius at the age of nineteen. It was his combination of eye and brain that did it. Well—I spoke just now of dry-stone walling. The unbreakable rule in competition walling is that your waller must never change his mind about a stone, once he has it in his hands. When he's picked it up, that must be the next one he uses. He must measure it first with his eye. He isn't allowed second thoughts.

'And Jonathan was the same with a piece of wood. Wood did what he wanted it to. He never made a drawing. In the early days, he used to drive me to distraction, because I couldn't get him to take a measurement. It took me a long time to realise he didn't have to. He just knew. He saved me a small fortune, when I come to look back on it—not just for knowing where to cut, but for seeing in advance what could be made from what was left.'

He picked up a tenon saw and looked critically along the set of its teeth.

'But he never wanted the work. The first few weeks he was with me, I didn't talk to him much. After that fight with Stanley Redfern, I left him to find his own feet. I used my eyes and ears and gave him a chance to show himself. Then one day, coming back from a flooring job we were doing at Nithen End, I asked him how he thought he was making out.

' "You've made your mistakes," I said. "We all do. A man who doesn't make a mistake the first time he does a job, might as well have left that job alone. You'll make a carpenter."

' "Don't want to make a carpenter," he said.

'I didn't answer him. It was best not to hear that kind of talk.

' "In any case," he said. "What carpentry do you ever let me do? All I'm ever set on is pushing the hand-cart or sweeping the floor."

'So I told him, "You'll have to go on sweeping the bloody floor a while yet, you know. We all have to start with sweeping the bloody floor. Most important job in the bloody shop, sweeping the bloody floor. Somebody slips and breaks his bloody neck on a sawn-off corner, and then where are you?"

'Mind you, Mr Bailey, I know how it was with Jonathan Bonsall and his carpentry. Sentiment again. The way it had been put to him, the way they sent him off that farm, his carpentry was to be a punishment. He was ashamed of it—and that's something he never did get over. He felt like one of these Chinese criminals you see in magazines, with a damned great board round his neck to tell the world what he'd been up to. Sentimental fool.'

It was an angle on Jonathan Bonsall that I had not thought of. But I did not see how it would help me to further Jonathan's interests. It did not prove that he had not killed the woman; it did not suggest that he was unlikely to have done. Jonathan might well be a sentimental fool, but he was all too likely to do his sentimentalising after the event.

Joshua Mycock went on talking.

'Take his poaching. He never knew when to stop. I'd suggested to him, when I saw which way his talents lay, that I could dispose of a carcase or two to our mutual advantage. I knew a poulterer, back of Hollins Street, who could dispose of what we could let him have. So I started making things easy for Jonathan. If he got lost for an hour or two, in the hills near a job we were doing, I didn't ask questions. If he was out before dawn, going round his snares, I'd stretch a point if he was late for breakfast. Then one morning there was nothing in the shed. I laughed, later on, when I found out why. It seems he'd set his traps over Gadley way, out towards Cold Springs. But there was a circus billed to put its tent up on Fairfield Common and that morning, just as he happened up past Watford Farm, this procession came in sight down Long Hill. He wasn't expecting it, and he didn't know what it was about. All he saw was one elephant on the skyline, no keeper—I reckon the attendant must have been on the other flank—and the rest of the parade hadn't come in sight yet. Then this creature raised its trunk and trumpeted. I don't know what the cross-country record time is, from Cold Springs back to Buxton, but Jonathan must have broken it, that morning.

'But I didn't know why he'd let me down. So I pulled his leg a bit, and I saw that look cloud his eyes that I knew by now spelled trouble. He went to the circus that night, with Stanley and one or two others from the shop, but he broke away from them after the show. He came back here, got out the hand-cart, did the circle of the hills: Corbar, Fairfield, Staden, Grin, Edgemoor—all his haunts, and everybody else's, too. Every keeper's traps—and nearly every poacher's. It was his handiwork that night that made MacTaggart swear he'd get him. And there was another keeper, back of Ladmanlow, who was breeding from a covey in his own wood yard. How many times the young bugger came back here that night, I don't know. How he got in and out without waking us, still beats me. I reckon if he'd fancied burglary, he'd have made a go of it.

'Breakfast time, and he's punctual at table. Ate like a bloody hyena. Had nothing to say for himself, behaved as if he'd defaulted again. So much so, I had a quiet word with him—half comic, you know. "You're hardly earning your keep this week, Jonathan."

'"Go and look in the shed," he said. "You'll see if I'm earning my keep."

'I didn't go specially to look. It never paid to seem to be eating out of Jonathan's hand. I thought there might be a rabbit or two, a brace of birds. When I'd been across the yard, after my second cup of tea, I pushed the shed door open. There were something like eighty rabbits and three dozen pheasants.

'"Christ!" I said. "And what do you think I'm going to do with that bloody lot? There's a difference between scratching your arse and tearing it."

54

'I did hardly any other work that morning—bar coming and going, getting rid of that lot at some sort of price.'

Was it, I thought, so far a cry from that massive operation to a sudden swing of the axe at the woman he had not expected to meet in the yard of the *Little Rose*?

Joshua Mycock scratched his nose with his thumb-nail. He seemed to have read my mind.

'Mind you, what I'm telling you about happened all of thirty-five years ago.'

'And has he changed as much as that, in this intervening time, do you think?'

Mycock sighed heavily. 'We none of us like to think we've got a murderer in the family.' Then he made himself brighten up. It sounded very artificial. 'If anyone can get him off, you can, Mr Bailey.'

Quite useless flattery. How could Joshua Mycock know what I was capable of? In any case, I wasn't a criminal lawyer. My sort of work did not interest the daily press. Mycock was in no position to judge it. And I think he saw this as soon as he had spoken. I carried no magic with me.

'You don't exactly look as if you're about to explode with encouragement, Mr Bailey.'

'Something very unexpected will have to turn up before I can do that.'

'You mean all you can hope to do is try and keep him quiet at his trial? Help him get through it with as little misery as may be?'

Joshua Mycock was a man of unencumbered, if unexciting vision. I always had thought so. I did not think that he was being less than realistic now.

CHAPTER FIVE

To bring myself to call on Alice Bonsall, I had to appeal uncompromisingly to my own sense of duty. Since I was the only hope she could turn to, I could only expect her to do so with inflated, heart-breaking faith.

Deeply sympathetic eyes: a flutter of white apron-ribbons across the lawn at Corbar Edge Hall. What she had handed Jonathan Bonsall on that occasion had been a packet of pastries from the kitchen; an impulse to do something for a begrimed and injured boy. A gesture that had anchored her for the rest of her life.

She was resting on her sofa when I knocked. The clothes she was wearing about the house were black and unshapely: the remnants, actually, now taken into everyday use, of the mourning she had bought for her father's funeral, twenty years ago. The house had that look about it that rooms bear when a large and impoverished family has left the nest. Two of the girls were still at home— I did not inquire where they were that afternoon. I had lost track of the remainder of the family, but worked it out— I think I was correct—that there were two children still at school under the latest Education Act.

For the rest it was a household of cushions worn thin, of lace curtains that had been washed a dozen times too many, of worthless and cherished trinkets, of large framed photographs of her parents and Jonathan's. It was within my memory that the fruits of photography had first come the way of ordinary people; it was an important feature in their lives.

Alice Bonsall set the kettle on the hob. I would have to take tea with her. Like so many of her kind, she had brought into her cramped, over-furnished, scrupulously clean little home as much as she could of the grace of the great houses in which she had worked.

'Mrs Bonsall, I hate to take your mind over all this misery again. But there are things I need to know.'

I had been meeting Jonathan Bonsall almost every week-end at the time when he set out to court this girl. And then, when he started paying attention to her in earnest, I sometimes did not see him for a month or two at a time. He had never described her to me directly, but I had learned a lot about her in an oblique fashion. I had found it amusing to watch from a distance which way things were going; and I felt a little melancholy about it, too, for I could see that I had almost lost his company already.

She had given him pastries and he had at first seen no way of contriving to meet her again. For two or three weeks he devolved into the mooning stage; it must have been as apparent to his mates in the workshop as it was to me in our coverts and on our river banks.

Then, in characteristic Bonsall fashion, he had struck a blunt blow. Alice Offord answered the door-bell at the Hall and was horrified to see in broad daylight, grinning at her nervously, the boy they had had on trial in the library; horrified, because if MacTaggart or the Sergeant-Major had caught sight of him, there was a likelihood of more blood and bruises.

'I've come for my cap,' he said.

'They'll give you cap if they set eyes on you.'

The R.S.M. had knocked the thing from his head in the boiler-room, preparatory to left-wheeling him in front of the G.O.C.-in-C.

She darted indoors and brought it for him. She had washed it, though there was a grease-patch that would not come out, had stuffed the lining in as well as she could and sewn up the rents.

'Mrs Bonsall,' I said. 'It must have been against your

57

better judgement that Jonathan went down to the *Little Rose* to see your daughter-in-law.'

'I should never have let him go.'

'It was entirely his own idea, of course?'

'I should have gone with him. Or gone myself, alone.'

If Jonathan had never paid that call—if perhaps he had delayed it or advanced it by an hour ...

'It was his idea to go?'

'There were things she had that she had no right to. I mean, we'd given them things, as you would any couple setting up home. But we'd *lent* them things, too. There was a *jardinière* that had belonged to Jonathan's father—'

I knew these things were not trivial. There was hardly a family in the town, poor though some of them might be, who did not own an article or two that had been treasured over three generations: a clock, a warming-pan, a Queen Anne cupboard. Possessions. We lawyers lived on them.

'And there was a hanging lamp that had belonged to my mother.'

Alice Bonsall had crossed the girth of the country to enter into domestic service. She hailed from the Cambridgeshire marshes, and still had the East Anglian's melodic cadences in her speech.

'What are the Fens?' Jonathan had asked me, sharing my cold partridge and a bottle of hock in a shooting-butt on the heights of Over Haddon, and I knew that she had been opening the nostalgia of her heart to him. Samphire; what was samphire? There was a great deal of superstition, a lingering of witchcraft in the minds of the Fen Tigers, and she had filled him with strange legends that he did not understand. Later in life they had gone back for a couple of weeks every August to her native dykes and droves.

'He had promised he was not going to stir up trouble,' she said. 'He was going to put it to her that in all fairness there were things that we ought to have back. If she had thrown any difficulties in the way, then we would have come together to see you.'

What chance did they think I might have had of influencing Miriam Bennett?

'I promise you, Mr Bailey, Jonathan was not looking for trouble. That porter, on Derby station—that dreadful thing that happened. I know, whenever in his life Jonathan has done something terrible like that it has always quietened him down. He would be as good as gold for months, months afterwards. We had to have those things. They were our memory of Jonty. And if Jonathan went for Miriam, the way things look as if he did, then it must have been because of something that she said to him.'

So even Alice Bonsall had a little doubt in her mind. She did not want to believe it of Jonathan; but she did believe it.

Alice Bonsall was a devout—a limited, perhaps—but a sincere and utterly reliable woman. Indeed, Jonathan's first open meeting with her had been at the Wesleyan Chapel in the Market Place, where she sang in the choir, and where she was allowed to attend on Sunday evenings, provided the General was not giving a dinner-party. It says a great deal for the state Jonathan was in that he was able to sit through the long extempore prayers and the long comminations of every imaginable grade of mortal sin without as much as a fidget.

Ironically enough, their second meeting had been in Anglican precincts. Alice had said to him—almost with fear about its implications—that she expected he was Church, not Chapel. And Jonathan nodded vaguely: he presumed he was. So she said that next Sunday it was only right that they should go to his place of worship instead of hers. He had agreed, without any thought about it at all and was caught without counsel when they met in Higher Buxton a week later and she had remembered. She had brought with her a bunch of flowers from the

Hall, a decoration for the Wesleyan altar-table.

'But I expect they'll be glad of them in your church, too.'

He took her to St Anne's at the top of Bath Road, because it was the nearest. But the floral arrangements had already been completed by a committee of women. And a sidesman had to turn them out of someone else's rented pew. Neither of them liked the church nor its Evensong. They found the gloom of the low rafters oppressive; there was none of the heart-on-sleeve fellowship of the free churchmen; neither of them knew their way about the Prayer Book. They could not even understand a pointed psalm.

Afterwards he walked her back to Corbar Edge by a very circuitous route.

'Jonathan's a nice name,' she said. ' "Shall Jonathan die, who hath wrought the greatest salvation in Israel?" You're what they call a poacher, aren't you, Jonathan?'

'I always say that God's creatures are his gift to the world at large.' This was a quotation from his cousin Joshua's philosophy.

'But it isn't right, really. One of these days you're going to find yourself in real trouble.'

'I can run. I'm not scared of MacTaggart.'

'But that's not what really matters, is it, being afraid of Mr MacTaggart. And I *would* be afraid of him, if I were you. I've heard him say what he's going to do to you, if he ever catches you in the Warren again.'

And she told him about her home far away, where there were no hills and no moors and no rocks, but long straight miles of mud-coloured, weed-choked water, strawberry fields and plum and apple trees in their close-ranked thousands.

I jerked my mind back from memories of Alice in the happy past, to my reason for calling on her now.

'How long ago was it,' I asked her suddenly, 'that Jonty borrowed his father's axe?'

I could see that so material a reminder shocked her very close to tears.

'I should never have let him have it. If only I had never let it go out of the house! And Jonathan was so angry with me when he came home. I ought to have remembered how a man feels about his tools—especially when he's been trained in a workshop. He would never allow even our own boys to touch his chisels or his planes. Not even Jonty.'

'How long ago was it, Mrs Bonsall?'

'Two or three months.'

'Before he left Miriam, you mean?'

'That's right. He was going to hack out a sycamore stump in their garden.'

'I see. So he took it to the cottage, not to the *Little Rose*?'

'That's right. I would certainly not have let it go, if I had known it would be taken there.'

'I wonder how and why it was brought into town. In fact, it's never been exactly clear to me—'

I looked at her closely. She was such a good woman— and I am using the words in neither a satirical nor in a purely admiring sense—that there was a range of subjects that I found it genuinely embarrassing to discuss with her.

'I have never properly understood why Jonty abandoned the cottage and took lodgings—since Miriam had gone back to the *Little Rose*. I would have thought that he was more than capable of seeing to himself.'

'He was, Mr Bailey. But Miriam stayed on at the cottage for a week or two after he left. She was only going to the *Little Rose* in the afternoons, at first. I suppose she got tired of moving between one place and the other.'

In fact, Jonty might have been said to have driven her back to the Rose. And when things happened like that in Jonty's life, one was apt to think of them as intentional.

'I don't like talking about it, Mr Bailey.'

61

'Nor do I. But we can't afford to leave anything unlooked-at.'

'I know. And Walter's told me—now.'

She stopped talking to make the tea. She had rather a splendid pair of cups and saucers—lacking the rest of the set, of course, but Derby porcelain, hand-painted by Zachariah Boreman: Thorpe Cloud and the lower Dove below the stepping-stones, delicate in apple-greens, with the most ethereal of azure horizons. It was one of several things that had been given to her by the housekeeper when she had left the General's service.

At least, anything the inarticulate Walter might know, I could undoubtedly coax from at least half a dozen more voluble informants: Sam Critchlow, for example.

But Alice Bonsall, the topic once broached, was resolved not to shy away from it. She handed me a plate of jam tarts. She baked twice weekly, and her pastry always had been exceptional.

'Mr Bailey—she'd had a visitor at the cottage, perhaps more than one. But there's one we know about. While Jonty was working for her keep at the Town Hall.'

'I see. And Jonty knew about this?'

'I don't see how he could help but know. I think he was one of the last to find out about it—when it was on the tongue of everybody else in the town.'

The front door opened and one of her daughters came in. Oddly enough, I cannot now remember whether it was Edith or Martha.

Alice Bonsall dropped her voice. 'Mr Bailey, after that —knowing what had gone on in the house—Jonty couldn't have stayed, could he?'

The young woman came through the room. 'Hullo, Mother. Good afternoon, Mr Bailey.'

'You do know what I mean, Mr Bailey?'

Edith—or Martha—went through into their little scullery.

'His own bedroom, Mr Bailey—'

'Yes, Mrs Bonsall.'

'There's never been anything like this in our family, Mr Bailey, not on either side.'

'I'm sure. And do you happen to have heard—?'

She put her hand on my arm.

'Is there a Mr Weigall, Mr Bailey? A Mr Roger Weigall? Who comes from Leicester?'

CHAPTER SIX

Of course I knew Roger Weigall. He was the one after Stephen Stanhope, before Andrew Wilson.

But I must avoid giving the impression that Miriam Bennett was a blindfold human flail in a china shop of men's hearts. She did break some; but if she had not had it in her to do that, she would not have charmed others. It was not entirely her fault if men lost (or found) their sense of proportion before her. And the quiet observation which some of us kept was as innocuous a parlour game as was ever played on the back benches of the *Little Rose*.

But we could afford to be more detached in our observation than could Mabel Mosscrop. She had to be as assured as she was unobtrusive, as ready to pounce as she was careful to remain in ambush. Mabel Mosscrop cannot have doubted that one day, sooner or later, she would lose Miriam Bennett. There were a number of ways that this could happen, some of them less acceptable than others. And it was not merely that Mrs Mosscrop wanted a decent return on her expenditure of capital, and that over a not unreasonable period of time. There was a sincere relationship between the two women. One could safely call it maternal: in its hatred as well as its love.

If only, some of us thought, in our moments of idler speculation, the status quo could be maintained for another six or seven years. Within that time, Jack Mosscrop would be gathered to his fathers on an alcoholic vapour. Miriam Bennett could be carried off by some wealthy princeling, prostrate with devotion and profoundly kind. Sam Critchlow could marry Mabel; and the *Little Rose* could carry on, if not as before—for that was regrettably inconceivable—at least without breaking faith too harshly with its true dependants.

In this finely poised context, the business with Stephen Stanhope brought nothing but innocent and nostalgic pleasure to any of us except, for a few melancholy days, to Miriam herself. *A debonair and gentle tale of love and languishment.* It was idyllic while it lasted, and we harder-bitten ones, in our remoter corners, could afford to enjoy the idyll, because we had no fears that it might last.

Stephen Stanhope was immature and harmless, a sheltered adolescent in his outlook, though he had already reached his mid-twenties. He was staying in Buxton with his parents. His father was a vaguely sick man, cosseted in shawls and scarves, who hardly ever left his over-heated hotel, where he was said to be engaged on the memoirs of his services to the Queen at trading posts in torrid climates. His mother was a massive and energetic woman who had found herself an unexpected niche amongst the missionary sponsors of one of the Buxton churches. Perhaps she was trading on her reminiscences of cannibalism in the European hill settlements whilst her husband was sweating it out down-river.

Stephen was a lonely man who occupied himself largely in geological field expeditions. We gathered that he was better informed than many amateurs though not, we suspected, deeply scholastic. He discovered the *Little Rose* by accident, and Miriam Bennett inevitably. He involved her in long conversations across the beer pumps, in which we caught words like foraminifera, encrinites and trilobites. The first time he invited her to accompany him on one of his outings, she was uncertain whether to accept, fearing boredom more than the honour of his intentions. Miriam felt under no personal compulsion to improve her knowledge of the age of the rocks. But Mabel encouraged her—almost pushed her into the assignation—and Sam Critchlow thought that a day in the open air would put a touch of needed natural colour into her painted cheeks.

One picnic led to another. Miriam was generously treated in the matter of free time, provided she was back in time for the main business of the evening—and did not miss any appointments with hairdresser or dressmaker. She came back with samples of Blue John from the Winnats, galena from Oxlow Rake, Hoptonwood marble from Wirksworth and barytes from the *Via Gellia*. She had her moments of disappointment, too. She picked up a specimen that she considered particularly beautiful from the ballast behind Alsop-en-le-Dale station, only to be told in cavalier fashion that it was a mere lump of London and North Western Railway clinker.

Their companionship was not sexless—far from it. But they were both young—each of them in a different way—and realistic conceptions of sexuality were barely rippling the surface of their consciousness. Perhaps also the little hammers, the field notebooks, the little bags and boxes for their findings, which they carried with them everywhere, acted as a further obstacle against those accidental physical contacts with which trouble often starts.

We did not, of course, spy on them. I find it difficult to explain how we came to know as much as we did about what was going on between them. We relied very heavily on our imaginative reading of the signs, prompted by experience in a wide variety of backgrounds.

Then one evening Miriam came back amongst us more pensive than usual. She seemed unusually disinclined to talk—and about the day's excursion not at all. And Stephen Stanhope, having delivered her to the door, did not stay for his usual modest *Vino da Pasto*. We held various theories, all of them sympathetic, but Mabel Mosscrop, who knew, did not pass the word round that day. Stephen Stanhope had asked Miriam to marry him.

It was not to be considered a practical proposition. As far as we were aware, the Stanhope parents had not even met the girl. We did not know what their resources were, but they gave the impression of comfort without surplus. Stephen did not appear ever to have done any work or to have been trained for any. We fancied that there might be some history of real or supposed delicacy and we were not disposed to let our Miriam go to an impotent. The very conception of his proposal was an indication of his immaturity.

Miriam, conventionally, asked for time to consider. Stephen had at least the sincerity to ask her not to keep him waiting too long. She promised him that he should have his answer at a Pavilion concert to which he had invited her later in the week.

We heard the outcome in the course of time. I do not know how seriously she was tempted. A first proposal must certainly have given her a great deal to think about, even if she did not think it worth serious consideration (which I doubt, since I think that, with reservations, she had become genuinely fond of the young man). I do not know how directly Mabel Mosscrop dared to advise her. And I hardly think that Sam Critchlow kept his opinions to himself.

I do remember that we had an evening with Mabel behind the bar whilst Miriam was listening to excogitated *fughettos* by some obscure and now forgotten Austrian composer who had come to conduct his own work. And I do know that she came back unaccompanied shortly after ten o'clock, flushed and silent, and went straight up to her room.

The explanation was that during the interval, while they were stretching their limbs along the palm-lined glass corridors, Stephen began to behave in an untypical manner, abrupt and ungallant, ushering her through a side-door into the open air, as if he had caught sight of someone from whom he wanted to hide her. Miriam was at once on her intuitive mettle, sniffing her surroundings for danger signals like an animal that scents an unfamiliar threat. She unmistakingly spotted the reason for Stephen's apprehension: an imperious woman riding the billows of the promenading concert-goers like a clipper in negligible seas.

Stephen tried to retain her, saying something about wanting to make opportunity to talk to his mother first. Miriam sailed through the turnstile into the night. A few days later an obsequious representative called at the hotel and wanted her to sign a paper in exchange for a once-and-for-all payment of fifteen pounds. I was not called upon to advise her. She refused either to touch the money or put her name to the renunciation.

So much for Stephen Stanhope. Roger Weigall was a very different proposition. More than one of us was worried by Roger Weigall—and more than one of us had plans ready in case Weigall's activities needed any counter.

The crisis came at a more or less private party very late one night when the doors of the *Little Rose* had been ostensibly bolted. Such revelry—from which strangers and comparative strangers were diplomatically excluded—took place in the inn from time to time after the last member of the casual public had gone on his way. I would, I suppose, have been made welcome at any of these gatherings, but I usually contrived to evade an invitation. The parties were harmless enough, but the noise and familiarity were hardly in my line. On this occasion, however, I could scarcely have stood out from the merriment without appearing positively curmudgeonly. I was staying at the *Little Rose* for a few nights whilst new gas-fittings were being laid in my home, and I could not have withdrawn without seeming supercilious.

Sam Critchlow was there. I remember he sang a ballad called 'My old man's a fireman on an Elder-Dempster boat'. Whatever other qualities his voice lacked, volume was not amongst them. He was, I think, conditioned to compete with a *continuo* of North Sea gale.

Mabel and Miriam came and joined us on the public side of their counter. Jack Mosscrop was in evidence: a great flabby belly, pores perspiring with sheer alcoholic weakness, his bespectacled moon-face grinning with outgoing good humour. He was the happiest and most benevolent walking suicide I had ever met, though I cannot imagine in what deep-dyed gloom he faced his morning wakening. Fortunately, this never happened early in the day.

But the couple who really set the tone of the party—in whose honour, I suspect, it had been arranged—were Jenny Everett and a man called Weigall whom she had with her.

Jenny Everett was a young woman in her raddled late twenties whose acquaintance I had till now scrupulously evaded. I can claim that I had never spoken to her in my life, and I was relieved that she did not seem to recognise my existence now. She was already too far gone in drink to take in a formal introduction.

It was certainly not Mabel Mosscrop's custom to extend the hand of fellowship injudiciously to society's less virtuous gleaners. It came as a surprise to me later when Police Inspector Brunt let it drop in conversation that she occasionally provided a plate of food on a corner of her kitchen table for a prostitute down on her fortunes on a cold, wet night; but I think that these were cases on whom she had taken individual pity. I do not know the origin of her relationship with Jenny Everett. She may have been a former *protégée* to whom she remained loyal in her charitable and forgiving way; perhaps some previous potential Miriam *manquée*—perish the thought—to whom the door had so far never been closed. I had only been coming to the *Little Rose* some seven or eight years myself.

At any rate, Jenny Everett had evidently worked in the house some time previously, and did so no longer. She had travelled hopefully; I heard Manchester mentioned, Sheffield and Nottingham. And now and then she had returned to the Rose, bringing with her a series of putative partners, on a scale of optimism which lost heart with the passing of the years. One of them, whilst the curve was still rising, is perpetually alleged to have been a baronet. But even Mabel Mosscrop's tireless match-making efforts had achieved nothing for her.

The latest on her devolutionary tree proclaimed the realistic adjustment of her sights. Roger Weigall had crisp, tight curls at the back of his head and a row of flat ones plastered down over his forehead. The black was generously peppered with grey. His shoulders were padded— there was all-round evidence of desperate effort behind his appearance. The cut of his suit was not quite fashionable enough, his waist not quite sufficiently contained in it. There was a significant cloudiness in the whites of his eyes. I have no doubt that there was one particular type of satisfaction that he could have given Jenny Everett, and that he would not have been loth to oblige her, had she remained sufficiently sober to afford minimal co-operation. Roger Weigall was, in fact, a commercial—though he could usually find some more imposing description of himself when he thought that his temporary social milieu would be happier with it. Commercials were rare in the *Little Rose*; Mabel Mosscrop's policy was to price them elsewhere; but a friend of Jenny Everett merited special treatment.

It soon became obvious that any effort on Jenny's behalf tonight was likely to be unproductive. There must, in fact, have been something fundamentally wrong with any man who persisted in his attention after such snubs and droolings as we had seen her deliver to Weigall. She was on the verge of becoming maudlin. She suddenly decided that she wanted to sing—and kept harking back to the idea in spite of all efforts to lead her away from it. Mabel Mosscrop was replenishing her glass with white wine of increasing dilution.

As a party, this was now too embarrassing to be endured. Mrs Mosscrop looked at me apologetically. Her husband, totally insensitive to the undercurrents, began to try to alter Jenny's frame of mind with the sort of banter which would have done for normal circumstances.

It had been apparent for some time that Weigall had lost interest in Jenny. He was, however, now obviously aware of Miriam. There was no mistaking the single-mindedness of his glances. And, moreover, a perceptible change had come over his deportment at a noticeable moment in the evening. He began talking more loudly, not directly to Miriam, but clearly for her exclusive benefit, encouraged to further invention when she laughed immoderately at some of the things he said. I cannot remember any of his exact sallies—in any case, as witticisms, they are not worth recording; they were mostly concerned with his contempt for the undeserving people for whom he worked and his talent for scoring off them at every turn. He did not apparently recognise the presence in the room of any of us other males. If one of us spoke, he did not apparently hear us.

It is not surprising that he was struck by Miriam. Most newcomers into the *Little Rose* were. You could sense the halt in their speech and in the movement of their eyes, feel their momentary concern for the speck of dust on their lapel or the crookedness of their Marlow bows. Yet it is difficult to do justice to Miriam's beauty. She was wearing tonight a long gown of some lustrous material, deep coppery red to match her elaborate and meticulously piled hair, and set off by an imitation emerald brooch in the form of a sinuous lizard. At her wrist she was wearing a bracelet with a device then popular and known, I believe, as the *Love laughs at locksmiths* motif: twin heart-shaped padlocks transfixed by an arrow, from which dangled a key, a chain and a tiny golden ladder. Her skin was like mellow polished stone, which lent her features the serenity of sculpture. There was one tiny flaw in her appearance:

71

the very slightest twist in one of her front upper teeth. It seemed, somehow, to show that she was human after all.

In the management of her bar and those who frequented it, she was a goddess undisputed. But when it came to larger issues, her mental grasp was, I fear, limited to the superficial and the fleeting. She had evolved for herself a manner of speech that was a compromise between the purity of her local vowels and the drawl of a characteristic visitor. I found it extremely restful, even, dare I say it, musical. But the things that she had to say were rarely of consequence, limited as they were to the gossip of the circle and to repetitions of other people's successful saws. She was, therefore, very easily impressed by Weigall's brand of self-advertisement. For a second time she laughed cacophonously at something he said, and Sam Critchlow tried to divert her attention by calling over to her that he had had a letter that morning from his daughter in Port Said. This was an element in a complex range of legends which Critchlow had invented about himself. He never spoke about the conventional wife in every port, but the waterfronts of the world appeared to be generously populated by his offspring—daughters, never sons—who kept up a prolific correspondence with him.

Miriam hardly heard him now; she acknowledged with a movement of her head that she knew he had spoken to her; and she made it clear that this was not the topic of the moment. Roger Weigall got up from beside Jenny and walked towards her table. She started to hook out a chair for him with the point of her foot, an inelegant gesture, and was quite unsuccessful in the manoeuvre, which compelled him to stumble forward almost urgently to her assistance.

It was at this moment that Jenny Everett opened her eyes—she had fallen into a befuddled doze and her whole bearing was disorganised—and, to my horror, she caught sight of me. I am not at all cut out for graceless female

72

company, and I always fare badly if I allow myself to fall into it. She patted with the flat of her hand the chair that Weigall had left. As well as I could, I signalled in gentlemanly fashion that I declined, but that I did not wish to appear unfriendly; but I think I probably shuddered visibly. Mabel Mosscrop got up and went and sat on the chair in question. I picked up my glass. Thomas Hardy's *Hand of Ethelberta* was waiting on my bedside table.

Sam Critchlow was watching me closely, and beckoned me over to him. 'You're staying here the night, aren't you, Mr Bailey?'

'I am indeed.'

'Keep your eyes and ears open for that bugger.'

He nodded towards Weigall, who was pouring Miriam her second glass of Offley's tawny port.

I wished them all goodnight.

So Weigall had been to visit Miriam at the Bonsalls' cottage up on Burbage Edge, and had begun to drop in at the *Little Rose* again since the beginning of Jonty's prison sentence?

It was clear that I was going to have to face up to the sort of confrontation which I normally do all I can to avoid. It is not by accident that I have chosen to specialise in that branch of the law that does not bring me up unnecessarily against members of the public. But I can always bring myself to do what has to be done. After I had left Alice Bonsall, I went to my office to see whether anything of interest had arrived by the afternoon post. And I was delayed for an hour by a vexatious query that had come in from the Midlands about a dubious restrictive covenant on a property that a manufacturer of power-lathes was buying.

When I reached the *Little Rose*, the hostelry was almost deserted. It was that time of day between afternoon tea and the hour of the apéritif when there was hardly any business. Roger Weigall was not there: out, I supposed, filling his order book by strokes of genius with which he would strive to impress us later on. Even Sam Critchlow's pewter tankard was hanging idle on its hook. There was only one drinker in the bar, a rather shabbily dressed man with sparse hair brushed laterally across a bald patch, and pipe ash spilled down the front of his coat. He had at his left hand an almost full glass of brandy and water, which he appeared to have forgotten, and at his right an open novel, with a strip of frayed leather as a bookmark.

'Police Inspector Brunt,' Mabel Mosscrop whispered to me. I had had to wait for her to come to the bar from her private quarters.

'I know.'

But we had never seen him here socially before.

'He's been here an hour or more. Says he's not here on duty; says it's for pure pleasure. He doesn't look to me as if he's getting much.'

I looked sideways in his direction. He was absorbed in his book. He did not appear to be aware that I had come in.

'I don't understand it, Mr Bailey. As far as he's concerned, the case is finished, isn't it?'

'For some policemen, no case is ever finished.'

'He didn't say anything to me about it, but he gives me the feeling that he isn't satisfied.'

'You know very well that I'm not satisfied, either.'

She mixed me my *Sangaree*, which I carried over to a corner where the man could catch my eye if he wanted to.

He waited until I had settled myself, turned the page to finish the paragraph he was reading, then smoothed down his bookmark, closed the volume, pushed his glass disdainfully away from himself and looked directly at me.

CHAPTER SEVEN

It was after I had talked to Police Inspector Brunt that I made up my mind to write down the story of these events. It was largely, I suppose, because I wanted to relive them. No, *relive* is the wrong word. For too many men, to relive their lives would be a self-inflicted cruelty. *To try to understand* would be a better term, and that must involve using one detail to recall another. The tendrils of cause and effect span the generations.

Jonathan Bonsall was fretting at the rhythm of the long prison day, and the even longer prison night, because someone had taken the edge off his axe.

Someone had taken the edge off his axe because his son Jonty had died of pneumonia in the hospital wing of the same prison.

Jonty had died in the prison hospital because his marriage to Miriam Bennett had failed.

And Jonty's marriage to Miriam had had to fail. That had been determined by what Jonty was, by what Jonathan and Alice had made him.

Police Inspector Brunt closed his book and looked over at me. By an exchange of facial expressions, I invited myself over to his table. He seemed so firmly established there, whilst I had barely settled at mine.

There were conventions between us that had to be made plain as a preliminary. Inspector Brunt had to let it be known that as a policeman he favoured a purely one-way traffic in confidences. And I had to show that this applied equally to a solicitor.

'You can hardly expect me to summarise the arguments of the defence, just in order to reinforce the prosecution.'

Inspector Brunt had a habit of making a long pause before his major pronouncements. It gave two different kinds of impression: firstly that he was thinking very deeply before committing his opinions to the dangerous tangibility of words; and secondly, as often as not, that the whole process had failed, and that no words were going to materialise after all. And then, when one had almost given up hope, would come the words themselves: unexpectedly flat, unemphatic—yet final.

The process took place now. I began to think that he had not heard what I had said, and I was about to repeat myself when he spoke.

'But then, I am not the prosecution. The prosecution is not in my hands. I am concerned only with events.'

'Events can be elusive,' I ventured.

This he ignored. Presently he embarked upon what seemed to be the second half of his statement.

'If I were in your position, Mr Bailey, I think I would be a very worried man.'

Another pause; presumably to disturb me.

'Indeed?'

'On behalf of your client, I mean.'

'I have already pointed out to you, Inspector Brunt—'

But this time he came back without hesitation.

'I am not trying to pry into your secrets, Mr Bailey. If you have any ...'

'Aren't you rather forgetting yourself, Inspector?'

'What I am trying to say is that you must be conscious of weaknesses in your case.'

'That is for the jury to determine.'

Compared with his previous performance, this had been almost a staccato exchange. But now he sat for many long seconds in uncommunicative contemplation. Yet he did not have the features to suit such an oracular display. He had a round, flaccid face, asymmetrically scattered with Cromwellian warts and pimples. There was no promise

76

of intellect in his eye, which was so watery that it looked as if it might be defective in even material vision. The only positive quality which the man seemed to have was patience. And I cannot see that patience is a virtue unless something worth waiting for lies at the end of it.

'Granted,' he said at last.

'We see eye to eye on that, then.'

His hands were lying on the table, palms downward, quite motionless, geometrically parallel to his book.

'But no defence, Mr Bailey, could be nearly as effective as a withdrawal of the prosecution.'

This time it was my turn to weigh up alternative sets of words.

'Is there some likelihood, then, that the prosecution is going to be withdrawn?'

'I am not saying that, Mr Bailey. I am not saying that. You must not quote me as saying that.'

'I don't find myself under strong compulsion yet to quote you as saying anything,' I said. 'I don't, in fact, find myself in very confident grasp of anything you *have* said.'

Thereupon he smiled—a transfiguration of his features that can only have been brought about by some hidden source of spontaneous pleasure.

'Ah, well, sir—we won't go at each other's throats as if we stood before the bar of a court. Just in the bar of the *Little Rose*, eh, Mr Bailey?'

I really could not bring myself to share his chuckle.

'What I am trying to say, Mr Bailey, is that Bonsall's best defence would be an alternative arrest.'

'And you envisage such an arrest?'

'Far from it, I am afraid. It's not just a question of putting two and two together. But two and two and two and two and two...'

Should I feign irritability and demand that he start talking in plain and common terms? Should I simply wait until he had completed his ritual preamble and felt ready to be explicit? Or might this never happen?

'I look on it this way,' he said. 'A man finds a dead body, and beside it an axe. He sees that it is his own axe, so he picks it up and looks at it. Then, seeing that it has been damaged by rough usage, he complains.'

'Yes. And that is what seems to me...'

'It seems to *me*,' he said, almost rebuking me for having any view of my own, 'to be so true a story—and yet so unlikely a one—that a man would be hard put to it to invent it.'

'Therefore?'

'Therefore, unfortunately, Mr Bailey, nothing. Or next to nothing. Except, perhaps, that the yard behind this inn is as accessible as a market place. And that when he stepped out into it, Bonsall had not, by anybody's showing, any reason to expect to find the woman there. It seems perhaps an elementary and futile piece of reasoning: but, assuming that Bonsall did kill her, she must have been alive when he came upon her. Alive, fully clothed, and wearing the full range of her everyday cosmetics—some of which had been transferred to the damaged blade of the axe. Whereas Bonsall had been firmly told that she was upstairs, distressed, and resting in her room.'

'You mean...'

'I have examined the landlord's wife on the subject of this anomaly, and she has shifted—or at least developed—her original statement. She now explained that she knew very well that the younger Mrs Bonsall was not in her room, but that this was a subterfuge to prevent the two from coming together.'

'It seems to me...'

'A legitimate, indeed a prudent manoeuvre. Mrs Mosscrop protests that she was not thinking in terms of actual violence. All she was anxious to avoid was an unpleasant scene—undesirable as that would be for the reputation of an inn that she likes to have considered as well-kept.'

'It certainly is that,' I said.

Inspector Brunt went into another of his brief sessions of cerebration. When he emerged:

'You know these people pretty well, do you, Mr Bailey?'

'I would say so. I have been coming here regularly for several years.'

'And what do you make of them?' The question was put so frankly that it verged on the impertinent. But there seemed no point in my becoming querulous.

'That is an enormous question,' I said.

'I will be more precise. We can take them one at a time. Mrs Mosscrop, for example?'

'An excellent landlady, a warm-hearted woman. A tremendously hard worker...'

'And anxious, you believe, to maintain an orderly house?'

'Inspector Brunt, if this were not an orderly house...'

'You would describe her, perhaps, as a motherly soul?'

'I think she mothers us all.'

'Especially motherly, would you say, to young women in a certain state of necessity?'

'I don't know to what extent she makes a habit of it.'

'Young women, for example, such as Jenny Everett, Kitty Brindley and Annie Brightmore?'

'I met Jenny Everett once unavoidably and briefly. I have never heard of the other two.'

'This man Critchlow...'

'The railway shunter...'

'I understand that he does make occasional appearances in the railway yards, and occasionally even makes a gesture towards a standing wagon with a brakeman's pole. He spends a good deal of his time in here, does he not?'

'He enjoys a drink.'

'And how would you describe his attitude to women?'

I resolutely steered myself away from absurdities. I hardly saw Brunt being amused by the tally of Critchlow's legendary daughters. But he misinterpreted my hesitation, and tried to come to my assistance.

'Would you, perhaps, describe his attitude as protective?'

'Inspector Brunt, what are you insinuating? This is a respectable house.'

'You are a man of the world, Mr Bailey?'

'I am a man of my own world.'

'A married man?'

'A bachelor.' I was prepared to dig in my heels if he attempted to become any more personal.

'I will concede, Mr Bailey, that this house has a respectable clientele. It seems to me, in fact, as an outside observer, that it has two planes of clientele. Which might well be a state of affairs that the management finds extremely convenient.'

I did not expostulate. I did not accept Brunt's implications, which doubtless derived from his long professional association with the seedy and unclean. But I saw no advantage in leaping to the defence of those whom he suspected.

'These men who were in the bar, for example, on the afternoon that the woman was killed: to which plane of clientele would you assign them? A Mr Roger Weigall, for example?'

'I was surprised to learn that he had returned to this vicinity.'

'Oh? Why was that?'

I did not want to become embroiled in the full unsavoury story. 'He did not behave well on a previous occasion when he was here.'

'What occasion was that, then?'

'Oh, a private party. He drank too much and became too interested in Miriam Bennett.'

'Too interested from whose point of view?'

'She was scarcely more than a girl at the time. We all felt concerned for her.'

To my relief, he did not follow this up.

'His interest in the young lady appears to have endured.'

'Yes. I heard he had called on her.'

But he did not appear to want to expand on this, either.

'There was another man present, too,' he said. 'A Mr Lowndes?'

'Yes. A young university historian, apparently a scholar of some calibre, though rather radical for my tastes. Someone told me he had been in. But I did not see him. I have not seen him since, oh, since the Bonsalls were married.'

'And there is yet another name—'

Brunt was unable to recall it, though this may have been one of the frequent acts of minor deception which he appeared to consider necessary. He brought out a notebook, and had some difficulty in orientating himself amongst its untidily written pages.

'Stanhope. Stephen Stanhope?'

'The geologist?'

'I did not know that about him.'

'But Stanhope left Buxton—when was it? 1901? 1902? Before the Coronation. He was a holiday visitor to the town.'

Brunt traced an entry with an unclean fingernail.

'We have established that he called on the younger Mrs Bonsall in her home about ten days after her husband went to prison. Two and two and two and two and two, Mr Bailey.'

'And two!' I said, foolishly. 'Deep waters, Inspector Brunt.'

'In which I had hoped you might be prepared to help me to dredge.'

'That is an unfortunate word, Inspector.'

'Murder is an unfortunate solution to some people's problems, Mr Bailey.'

We looked at each other, and I hoped that he judged the time ripe for another of his silences, for I would have liked a few minutes' thought myself. What had started out, on my part, as a not very hopeful attempt to exonerate Jonathan Bonsall, now looked as if it might possibly achieve its ends; but at what muck-raking cost?

I began to view the immediate future with distaste. But I had no intention, alone or in concert, of endeavouring to conceal the truth.

'—write it all down, Mr Bailey.'

I had hardly been aware that Brunt was still speaking.

'I was saying, Mr Bailey, that I hope you will be wholeheartedly with me in this extension of my inquiries. That you will try to remember everything—from years ago when these men and perhaps others—first appeared on the scene here. Anything. Any little triviality that you can remember may be the one that settles the whole panorama into place. And if I were you, I would write it down. Write it all down. That is the way to get one event recalling another.'

When he had done, I stepped out into Spring Gardens and bought myself a stout manuscript book bound in quarter leather.

CHAPTER EIGHT

1887 was the year of Jonathan Bonsall's majority; the year he came out of his time; the year of his masterpiece.

Over in Peak Low his father had surprisingly announced his intention of marrying again—an almost aggressively unattractive little spinster some fifteen years his junior, who was said never to have opened her mouth before her wedding, and never to have closed it again afterwards. Once given the keys of the farmhouse, she had demanded unthinkable structural changes. Everything had to be altered. Joshua Mycock was called in to advise on a new staircase, and after a few seconds' pondering, announced that the work would be left to Jonathan.

'It's a big job for a lad,' Jonathan's father said.

'He's not a lad any more. You're going to see something.'

Jonathan undertook the task without comment, exchanging no more than half a dozen sentences with his step-mother, and even fewer with his father. He listened without reaction to their suggestions, rejected most of them without saying that he was going to, and went about the work as he thought fit. Joshua came out only once whilst the work was in progress, but did not interfere, though he saw that the job was going to bear no similarity to its conception or its commission.

'No drawing?' he asked. And this was no longer an implied complaint.

'Got it in my head,' Jonathan answered.

The work took him a fortnight. Then without a word he left the house and wheeled the handcart six miles back to Buxton. His father rode over the same day, unstinting in his admiration.

'You'll be a master carpenter in your own right, if you keep on the right side of Joshua.'

'Not going to be a carpenter.'

He began to show Alice the paths about the hills. The Brigadier-General went to Harrogate for three weeks and she had more free time on her hands than she had ever had before. Mrs Maddock, the General's housekeeper, seemed to have taken a liking to Jonathan and made things easy for the couple. Jonathan mended sash-cords in upstairs windows and ate prodigious remnants of apple pie in the vast kitchen. Sometimes they walked on the fringe of Buxton's fashionable society, strolling along the High Path opposite Ashwood Park, even once paying at the turnstile and promenading sedately among the flower-beds of the Gardens, not questioning their inequality with the crinolines, the parasols and the croquet players. Once only, during one of their country walks, he stopped to pick up game, posting Alice on the skyline to watch for un-wanted comers. And on this occasion her unease communi-cated itself to him without the need for her to say any-thing He saw a rabbit's rump peeping up from one of his snares, but chose to pretend, for once, that he had caught nothing. There were unbelievable elements in his behaviour that summer.

Alice wrote a weekly letter home, though what she said in them about Jonathan was never made known to him or to his chronicler. It must have been informative—perhaps significantly more so than she intended. The result was an invitation for him to accompany her on her annual holiday.

It was the first time he had ever been more than thirty miles from home. He could not remain seated in the train. He had to stand by the window, afraid to miss anything at either side of the track. At Miller's Dale they had to change to the main-line train. And in spite of his attempt at masculine bluster, he was fretful and anxious. He was uneasy about the multiplicity of platforms, with their crates and trolleys, their milk churns and the Buxton visitors, returning with their trunks and leather hat-boxes.

But Alice was an old hand. She knew where to stand on the platform so that they could hope for an uncrowded compartment. South of Ambergate, the scenery was no longer familiar to him. Derby was his first sight of a red brick town, the Trent his first real river. London Road Station at Leicester was his first vision of a metropolitan hell, with clanging bells and gritty smoke billowing up under the floor-boards of the footbridge. They ate bread and cheese and slices of raw onion on a bench on one of the outer platforms.

After Peterborough stretched endless flat fields; orchards and farmsteads on the skyline, becalmed like the deckhouses of land-locked ships. Beds of bulrushes swayed out of ditches full of deep and still brown water.

Alice's father, who met them at Wisbech station in a trap drawn by an impatient chestnut gelding, was a man who had carried into his early old age the lean austerity of his harder years. He was neatly but not newly dressed, sprucely bearded and ramrod-spined. They passed a timberyard, pine resin fragrant in the hot sunshine, a Norwegian merchantman alongside a wharf, its rusting hull laid bare by the low tide.

'Your brother Ernest has taken services at Emneth and Fen End. He will be on full circuit after Michaelmas. Meg has a blue-eyed boy they have called George. "One generation passeth away and another generation cometh."'

The Offords' cottage was small, far away from other habitations, set in a clearing in a narrow orchard. Alice picked up a kitten.

'You must be one of Topsy's little ones.'

'To be sure! She can see the cat, but not her own mother!'

A little old lady, physically crabbed, who had retained vivacity of spirit if not of body after bearing sixteen children. For the space of a minute, Jonathan had no part in the reunion. Then Alice's father came forward to lead him into the cottage. Wooden chairs, with scarcely a cushion. A table laid ready for them, with white milk-cheese on a mat of straw, and a hunk of cold belly pork.

There were outings: to the samphire creek, where at low tide a horse and tumbril could be brought down to the water-line. They went by train to Hunstanton; bathing-machines with iron-rimmed wheels; shells and pebbles, starfish and shore-crabs; Jonathan had not seen the sea before. And there were relatives to be called on: they were made welcome on small holdings lost at the ends of over-grown fenland droves. Hands impervious to thorns were filling wicker skips with bushels of gooseberries.

One of Alice's uncles had a wagon-painter's yard; the artist's name in slender black paint on the glowing orange back-board of a hay wain. Jonathan picked up a spoke-shave and quietly finished a hub that was lying on a bench.

'Not looking for a job, are you, young man?'

'Got one. Going to be a gamekeeper.'

He helped another cousin, behind the grassy seawalls of the Nene Outfall, to repair crab pots with willow laths. And one night they had shrimps and prawns for supper. Alice's father held up a prawn to the evening light of the window.

'Esau!' he said.

Jonathan did not understand.

'He doesn't know his Bible,' the old woman said. She pronounced it to rhyme with *nibble*.

' "Behold, Esau my brother is a hairy man, and I am a smooth man." Genesis, 27: 11.'

He splayed out the legs of the creature to show Jonathan the hairy tentacles.

'You remember, Jonathan,' Alice said. 'How Rebekah sent Jacob to his father.'

86

Jonathan was reminded that tomorrow was Sunday, a prospect which even Alice found daunting. They had to be up with old Offord at four. He had seventeen miles to walk to the village chapel at which he was going to take the morning service. He proudly displayed his walking-stick and empty pockets.

'"Nothing for their journey save a staff only; no scrip, no bread, no money in their purse..."'

High summer bathed the Marshland lanes; peacock butterflies flitted about knapweed and ragwort; grasshoppers rasped in ditches; furry caterpillars crossed the flinty lanes on inscrutable pilgrimages.

There was Sunday school in another village, evening prayer in yet another. Then the old man suggested that as he was a slower walker than the youngsters, they might care to make their way back home ahead of him. For himself, he enjoyed solitude for meditation in the gathering twilight. Alice had codlin apples, bread and cold meat in her bag. They turned into an orchard and sat in the shelter of a hedge. Alice began to tell the strange legends of the Fens.

And Derbyshire had its superstitions, to be sure, but Jonathan listened to these as under hypnosis: medieval folk-memories of the Tigers and the Slodgers: Anglo-Saxon freedom-fighters taking refuge behind the fever-steaming reed beds; Black Shuck, a ghostly hound who padded about the droves and seawalls after dark, fore-telling pending death to anyone who met him.

Jonathan sometimes talked to me about that evening, but there were gaps in his accounts of it. But the tale most often told was how they had suddenly heard the snuffling of an animal's breath in the dusk, out amongst the long grasses between the seawall and the river's edge. They had seen bearing down on them the looming shape of some quadruped. Black Shuck? Immature and impressionable, they shared a moment of bleak terror. Then they identified a gypsy's horse, tethered with a swinging plank about his neck.

They laughed wildly. And a new sound bore down on them out of the night: an inescapable throbbing. The bell-note of iron bows breasting tidal water; red and green mast-heading riding lights, high in the darkness: a Swedish timber boat, hull and superstructure barely visible.

The couple's time in Wisbech drew to a close. The old man took Jonathan alone to show him his workshop in the Horse Fair: a saddlery—a pervading smell of saddle soap and old leather, of waxed twine and neatsfoot oil, of saddles soaked in the sweat of horses, of old timber and summer dust.

'How long is it now, Jonathan, that you have been walking out with Alice?'

'A year or more.'

'And you intend to marry her?'

'When I am settled in work and home.'

'You are a carpenter, and nearly out of your time?'

'Not going to be a carpenter.'

There was a significant pause. This was clearly a subject that had been talked out in the secret moments of the Offords.

'Going to be a gamekeeper.'

'Well, that's not a way of life that I know much about.'

However uneasy in his heart, the old man was never short of courteous.

'You will have no difficulty in being taken on?'

'I know where I shall be working.'

'And will it be easy enough, in your part of the country, to find somewhere to live?'

'I know where we shall be living.'

Jonathan did not tell Alice about this conversation. Their last Saturday came. The orange rolling-stock of the Midland and Great Northern Railway lumbered across the flat fields to Peterborough. The last of the reed beds gave way to hunting parkland, and after that the clangour and smoking hell of Leicester. Then, after the canal and black towers of Derby, the high sweep of hill above Darley Dale—dry-stone walls and squat, grey farm clusters.

A week after they arrived home, Alice came to see me in my office—wide, brown eyes, grieved and bewildered. Jonathan had disappeared. On the evening of their return he had carried her bag up to Corbar Edge and said good-bye to her at the lodge gates with an unimpassioned kiss. She had told him to meet her tomorrow evening in front of her chapel. But he had not kept that appointment. She had been to his cousin's house to ask for news of him, but Joshua knew nothing except that he had come in late on the Saturday, had gone upstairs without speaking to any-one, then left the house again. He had taken his suitcase and his best clothes. The box in which he was known to keep the shillings he saved had also gone with him. He had left no sort of message with anyone.

There was about Alice, in spite of her misery, a pretti-ness that I had hardly been aware of before. In her maid-servant's livery, insofar as I had paid any attention to her at all, I had thought of her only as a not unkindly en-slaved child. Now she looked a woman—and was conscious of it; but she stood only on the threshold of her woman-hood, utterly uncertain of her future. Idly, then, I won-dered whether she had come back from Wisbech pregnant: whether the sternness of her Methodism, the stoniness of Jonathan's innate puritanism, had yielded before a shared impulse that had become necessity.

Yet who was I to speculate? I turned my eyes away from her. I was too conscious, now, of that womanhood: the live hair stirring at her temple, the slender fingers, the contour of her breasts under the clean white imprisonment of her blouse.

89

I have so seldom been alone with a woman. I have been reluctant to allow it to happen. As I sit compiling this chronicle, I am reminded again of that night in the *Little Rose*, when Jenny Everett had drunk herself into a stupor and Roger Weigall had begun to make a set at Miriam. I had made good my escape, had said goodnight to them all, and no one had seemed surprised—or disappointed—to see me go. Mabel Mosscrop handed me a cheap metal candlestick in which lay a box of wax vestas. After the glitter of the bar, with its mirrors, its wrought-iron table-legs and its red plush, the inner regions of the *Little Rose* were gloomy and inhospitable. One felt that the house's only stairs were back-stairs. A single gas-bracket was burning at the head of the stairs, a bat's-wing jet, flickering blue with ragged yellow edges. I lay for a long time unable to find sleep.

I heard the remainder of the household come to bed; they were making no attempt to subdue their voices. There was the coarse laughter that often accompanies an awkward task: Jenny Everett was being carried to bed. I heard Jack Mosscrop belch. Roger Weigall wished them all a shoulder-slapping commercial's goodnight. Mabel Mosscrop and Miriam held a whispered conversation outside my door: probably housekeeping arrangements for tomorrow; I could not distinguish their words.

Still for a long time I lay awake. There were noises in the heart of the town: a gang from one of the less pretentious taverns kicking an empty can along a gutter; cats on a shed roof; the clank of couplings in the railway-sidings. Then I heard a single foot-fall on the landing, a hand brushing against a wall. And then the movement of feet a couple of furtive paces forward. I recalled what Sam Critchlow had said, downstairs in the bar, when he had spotted Weigall's interest in Miriam: *you're staying here the night—keep your eyes and ears open for that bugger.*

I got up and opened my door. The jet at the top of the

stairs had been turned down to a blue bud. Roger Weigall was in the corridor, carrying towel and soap, and wearing a velvet-lapelled smoking-jacket over his pyjama sleeping-suit. If he was pretending to go to the bathroom, I had caught him out; for he had already passed its door. He had to turn back to it when he saw me. I waited till he had shot the bolt behind him, then hurried to the short flight of uncarpeted stairs that led up to Miriam's attic.

I scratched on the panel of her door, afraid that I might waken everyone in the hotel if I knocked. There was no response: I tapped with my fingernails—and then again. I heard bare feet cross the room, and Miriam opened the door. When she saw me, she laughed.

'What's the matter, Mr Bailey, can't sleep?'

She was in a fine cambric nightdress with a wide hanging frill, its front embroidered and its cuffs trimmed with lace. She had let down her hair about her shoulders, which gave her a certain elemental look. The flame of the candle on her chest of drawers brought out its highlights in an almost breathtaking moment.

'Is there something I can go and get you, Mr Bailey?'

She was holding open the door about a couple of feet. I signed that I wanted to come in for a second. She moved aside to let me do so, closed the door behind us and stood with her back to it, looking up at me. And unexpectedly she giggled. She would be, I suppose, about eighteen or nineteen at the time. I was already in my forties. She probably thought of me as an old man already. I could see her slightly twisted upper tooth, the moisture on her lips, almost feel the warmth of her body welling out from her nightgown. My head swam.

In the distance we heard the flush of the water closet, then the opening and closing of the bathroom door again, the planting of a man's feet as he stood to listen. Then Weigall's steps disappeared towards his own end of the landing.

'I thought I ought to let you know,' I said. 'Our friend is on the prowl.'

She laughed again—and this time, so did I.

'Thank you for warning me. You had me worried for the moment. I thought you might be on the prowl yourself.'

It says much for the natural understanding between us that she could make a remark to me like that. But what a short-fall of understanding it was. It did not occur to her that in my comparative dotage I might also be a man with appetites that could be stirred. I had to get away from her—to run from the fragrance of her hair and the amusement in her eyes.

She stepped forward and opened the door with her hand behind her back. For a moment she came so close to me that her frills brushed my dressing-gown. And then I stepped past her, out on to the landing. I saw that she had a key on the inside of her door.

'If I were you, I'd keep that locked.'

'I will,' she said.

I walked halfway back to my room, but heard no turning of that key. I stood still and listened.

She must have been following my progress. I heard her lock her door.

CHAPTER NINE

I heard her lock her door.

I sat and wrote those words and laid down my pen beside the half-finished page. I had been writing faster, less carefully, in the last hour. My handwriting had become a negligent scrawl. An elliptical pool of light fell over my work—I was using the shaded oil-lamp over my desk rather than the gas-bracket on the wall, as I often do for more intimate tasks. Shadows deepened into the corners of the room, blurring the outlines of objects that I have at some time or other treasured: the replica of Beethoven's death-mask, the gold leaf on the green spine of Lyson's *Magna Britannia*. The embers of my fire collapsed into a feebly glowing cavern: I had forgotten to make it up, and I knew from weary experience that I would need half-an-hour on my knees to cajole fresh life into it. It was years since I had called for my factotum after half-past eight.

Suddenly I felt sour at the vanity of possessions. There was so much here that I had once been proud of: even a thing so trivial as my calabash in my oak pipe-rack with its college crest. But now, in the wake of Miriam's murder, and with Inspector Brunt prowling about with his insidious questions, I was sickened by the sight of everything. It suddenly seemed ironical that a few hours previously I had been preening myself on the pleasures and virtues of an evening spent at home; proud, even, of having stayed away for once from the *Little Rose*. Yet here I was already vaguely yearning for something that was missing, having to admit in all honesty that I missed the lights, the mirrors, the wrought-iron scrolls and the predictable conversation of my own little circle.

I was usually in my corner seat by a few minutes after nine o'clock. Tonight it was twenty minutes to eleven before I pushed open the frosted glass panels of the street door. The bar was full: I was aware as never before of the tumult of voices, the stale, hot and acrid smoke of cigars and pipes. My friends were in their places: the Borough Engineer, the proprietor of a prosperous bookshop and lending library, a fellow emeritus from an Oxford college who was engaged on an exegesis of Cotton's *Burlesques* that he surely never would finish: the *Little Rose*'s second plane. They had given me up for lost tonight. My usual chair had already been taken, but they began to re-arrange themselves as soon as they saw me come in.

I went up to the bar, which Mabel Mosscrop was managing alone. Her husband was standing near her, doing nothing, in smoking-jacket and cravat, swaying slightly on his feet and beaming genially on the company.

Then I saw that Police Inspector Brunt was also amongst the assembly, talking to Sam Critchlow, with whom he appeared to have entered into a blood brotherhood. He was cutting a very different figure from the laconic down-at-heel who had sat dropping pregnant hints to me in the dusky staleness of the afternoon. Then he had despised his own thin brandy and water; now he was quaffing from a quart pot of old and mild with a gusto to match Sam Critchlow's own. He was even laughing: great guffaws from his belly that shook the shoulders of his shabby overcoat. But when he turned his face in my direction, I saw that his eyes were still watery. A tear had actually formed, and was about to run down the flaky skin of his cheek.

He turned his face towards me, but might actually have failed to recognise me, so perfunctory was the interest he showed.

'Malta,' Sam Critchlow was saying. 'A trim little lady, that one. I have her photograph at home. I'll show it to you, some time. Mind you, last time I wrote to her, I tried to tell her a thing or two about sailors that she doesn't seem to have thought of.'

Inspector Brunt laughed as if he had been a life-long philanderer himself.

I carried my drink over to my friends' table, moving my chair at an angle so that I could keep the couple at the counter in a corner of my vision. From here I could not hear a word that they were saying, but I found an untold fascination in trying to guess what line Brunt was following. Presently Mabel Mosscrop, temporarily free from menial duties, moved down towards them behind her sinks and beer-engines, a light of merriment in her eyes, and was drawn into their conversation. Even Jack Mosscrop moved a side-step nearer to them, so that he could hear what they were talking about: which seemed to bring him a new source of pleasure, for the horizontal crescent of his great mouth gaped in new achievements of vacuity.

The talk at our table had turned to archaeology. Boyd Dawkins had unearthed a new Bronze Age Barrow, over towards Sawyer's Moss: a perfectly preserved skeleton in a sitting position, with its knees drawn up nearly to its chin. And that sent my mind off along another parallel and independent track, for it was near the crest of Sawyer's Moss that I had run young Jonathan Bonsall finally to ground when he had disappeared, long years ago, from his Alice's ken. I had been out for a walk with the General round his preserves. There had been a new outbreak of poaching on his estate, so impudent and on such a gluttonous scale, that the old man himself was out with reconnaissance and skirmishers in the hope of doing bloody battle.

I had suddenly caught sight of a wisp of blue woodsmoke over a curling lip of dead ground: the merest trace, suddenly vanishing, as from a fire quickly doused by a trespasser afraid of giving himself away. I said nothing about it. It crossed my mind—irrationally, but not in fact remote from probability—that Jonathan Bonsall might be the one who was watching us from cover not more than ten yards away. It was just the sort of neighbourhood in which he was likely to have gone to earth. But had he suddenly gone out of his mind? Was he tempting MacTaggart and Redbourne-Digby again? And if he still cherished hopes of being taken on as somebody's gamekeeper, did he think he was promoting his cause by this new onslaught against other men's game?

I said nothing: not because I felt myself committed to conspire with Jonathan in any circumstances that might arise, but because some streak of prudence determined me to find out what he was up to before I entered into the issue. In any case, I had nothing more than intuition to suggest to me that it was Jonathan who was involved here; but I felt pretty sure.

'I don't know how far I'm prepared to go with these archaeologists—'

The Borough Engineer was talking. I had lost the drift of their discussion.

'He finds an urn of calcined bones—little more than dust from a couple of thousand years B.C.—and tells us that it's the remains of a woman in early middle-age who was badly crippled by rheumatism.'

'That's Science for you.'

'Science! He seems to think he's Sherlock Holmes himself.'

This disparagement came from the retired academic.

Meanwhile, the official minion of the law, sartorially negligent almost to the point of actual squalor, was going great guns with his new friends. Their laughter reached us at our table over the vertiginous chatter of the bar.

Shortly after eleven, Inspector Brunt fastened his coat —I noticed that there was one button missing—and went home; or wherever it is that Inspectors of Police do retire at the end of their day. It seemed almost a telepathic gesture that communicated itself to all parts of the room. Other parties began to break up. By twenty minutes past the hour there were not more than half a dozen people left in the inn.

Normally, Mabel Mosscrop did not think of closing the house for the night whilst any customer was prepared to go on paying for hospitality in a serious way. If ever she did want to shut the place early—if she were exceptionally tired, or short of helping hands, or if there happened to be a knot of strangers present who were conducting themselves unattractively—then she had her own ways of discouraging guests from wanting to stay. Tonight she began a brisk and theatrical process of clearing up for the night—carrying trays of empty glasses to the counter and emptying ashtrays into a pail. One trio of visitors were impervious to such hints, and she began in a further corner to lift up the heavy, iron-legged chairs and stand them on the round-topped tables.

I signalled to her that I was ready to pay my dues, and she came over to me silently performing arithmetical calculations on her lips and the tip of her tongue. But instead of standing by my table in the usual way, making some cliché joke as she announced my indebtedness, she straightened the chair which the Borough Engineer had left and sat down informally at my side.

She was a big woman, and very strong. Her hands were large—as indeed was her entire physical frame. But with this went a certain classical handsomeness, an almost aristocratic simplicity that went hand in hand with her placidity and self-control. She was an Amazon: but essentially a feminine one.

I was surprised, though, to see her behaving in this manner. I could not recall that she had ever sat down with me before.

'I shall be glad when that policeman has stopped coming round, Mr Bailey.'

'He has his own station in life, like all of us. It gives him a job to do. Though I must say he looked to me as if his mind was a long way from duty tonight.'

'I never trust policemen,' she said.

'For my part, I haven't gone through life in such a way as gives me any reason to distrust them,' I answered. 'Nor, Mrs Mosscrop, have you, for that matter.'

I hoped she would not take that remark as too personal.

'It isn't that,' she said, and laughed, but not happily. 'I've not gone through life breaking the law. Not knowingly, anyway. It isn't the law that worries me. It's the other little things that get stirred up.'

She looked over towards the three others who still lingered. Their table was too far away for them to eavesdrop on our subdued talk; and in any case they seemed totally absorbed in a lively discussion of their own.

'And that Sam Critchlow—he's such a fool.'

I was surprised at the directness of this; but I thought she said it out of exasperation rather than malice.

'The things he was saying! Walking wide-eyed into every opportunity the policeman was giving him to put his foot in it.'

I thought carefully before I spoke. I had already sensed, from the way Brunt had talked to me this afternoon, that things were never again to be quite as we had known them in the *Little Rose*. I found in Mabel Mosscrop a great deal to admire; but I knew that I was going to have to be prudent about my allegiances in the muck-raking that had still hardly begun.

'About what kind of thing?' I asked, non-committally.

'About the old days.'

A convenient expression: it implied a way of life that we knew we could never recapture; but it implied also

98

that there was a past for which we had assumed we would never be held responsible.

'I can't think of anything in the old days of which you need be ashamed, Mrs Mosscrop.' And then I added, for the phrase suddenly struck me as unpardonably raw, 'Or even uneasy.'

'And indeed I haven't.' She spoke with consuming fervour. 'All I have ever done, Mr Bailey, is to make people happy; without doing anyone else any harm in the process.'

Well; quite. But there was an implicit admission here that *harm in the process* was capable of more than one definition, according to the standards of the observer. It was a silent admission, too, that Police Inspector Brunt could without difficulty harass the *Little Rose* on any number of nugatory counts.

'I'm worried about what's going to happen to Sam Critchlow, Mr Bailey.'

We, in the Rose, had always assumed that, like characters in the convenient context of a novel, Jack Mosscrop would eventually beam his moon-faced way into the grave, leaving Mabel Mosscrop and Sam Critchlow to marry after twenty years of mutual admiration. But I now saw that it was not going to be as simple as that. Since the middle of this afternoon I had looked at rather a large number of apparently simple things from a new and discomforting angle.

'Why? What do you think is going to happen to Sam, Mrs Mosscrop?'

'I think he's going to talk his way into the sort of trouble that he'll need someone like you to get him out of.'

One of the men at the other table looked over his shoulder at last, and Mabel Mosscrop went over to settle his account. And I was glad of the chance to try to marshal my thoughts: but I had not reached any satisfying conclusions by the time Mrs Mosscrop returned to me.

There was one question that I especially wanted to put to her, but I did not know how to frame it without risking a wholly wrong impression. What, seen through her eyes, had been Sam Critchlow's relationship with Miriam? I know that we had always looked upon him as a sort of fairy-godfather to her, in that more than slightly comic fashion that many men adopt when they are afraid that they might be laughed at for sentimentality. I was now beginning to understand, on this day of disturbing revelations, that this was a superficial view. The *Little Rose* was not a mere melodramatic peep-show, in which one was allowed to contemplate one's favourite illusions for the price of a glass of sherry. But I was not ready to believe that Sam Critchlow was a protector of women in that unsavoury sense that Inspector Brunt had insinuated. There must be some intermediate interpretation. Indeed, it had crossed my mind more than once that Sam Critchlow might have been grooming Miriam for his own personal purposes; which was not to forecast that he was likely to have things all his own way. This might explain why he had always been so correct with her whilst she was a child and a growing woman. Sam Critchlow had seen enough of life to have learned long-term patience; and he was not a man likely to derive satisfaction from anything less than maturity.

The other men left, and Mabel Mosscrop slipped a handful of coins into the pocket of her apron.

'Of course,' I said, 'we've all been thinking a great deal about Miriam, these last few days...'

But she misunderstood. She did not connect my line of thought with what we had previously been saying about Sam Critchlow.

'The time has come, Mr Bailey, for a minute or two's plain thinking about Miriam.'

She was going, I knew, to have to plod through all the sentimental preliminaries of respect for the dead. And after that, she was going to struggle to find a new set of propositions with which to try to quieten her own mind.

'Of course, Mr Bailey, she should never have married Jonty Bonsall.'

'With hindsight, we all know that. In Sam Critchlow's case, it isn't hindsight. He was outspoken.'

'And I wasn't. I won't say I encouraged them at first, for the simple reason that I didn't want to lose her from here. But when I saw that her heart was set on him, I shifted over to her point of view. As some mothers might for a daughter. I let myself be as blind as she was. But Miriam, you know—she wasn't a *bad* girl.'

This startled me, for she obviously meant the very opposite of what she was saying; and, deep in her mind, she knew that this was the case.

'She'd had a hard childhood. Her early years here weren't easy. She learned early on that there were two sides to men. Jonty Bonsall offered her something that is part of what every woman wants.'

'But only part? You'd know more about that than I do, being a woman . . .'

'And when she had that, and nothing else, it was all too tame for her.'

'I think I see what you mean.'

'Nobody's fault,' Mabel Mosscrop said, thinking tangentially. 'You can't go about giving other people orders about their lives; you might be wrong yourself. I'll admit that I hated losing her, when she did get married. But I knew that it had to happen one day. I didn't *own* her. But I was glad, too, when she came back here, first part-time and then full-time. Even though I knew in my bones that that was the beginning of trouble, real trouble. Let me get you another drink, Mr Bailey.'

'No, thank you. I must be on my way very shortly.'

'What was going on between Miriam and Jonty was not my affair. I told myself it was not my part to interfere.'

She might also have told herself that, like it or not, it was a soured relationship that was going to impinge on her own life sooner or later. But I did not breathe the thought. She was woman enough to see it for herself in her more honest moments. Mabel Mosscrop's chief guilt had been that she had taken refuge in an optimism in which she did not sincerely believe herself.

'All the same...' she said. Her eyes rested on me for a moment of personal searching, and I knew that under the pragmatism of her everyday life there was a persistent niggle of inconvenient conscience.

'I ought never to have let her find her way back into Roger Weigall's arms.'

I tried to be clever. 'It isn't only love that laughs at locksmiths. Lust finds a moment for a cynical little cackle, too.'

I do not know whether Mabel Mosscrop totally failed to understand, or was merely unimpressed.

'At any rate,' I added. 'I did put a barrier between that couple once. I have that satisfaction.'

'Oh, Mr Bailey? When was that?'

So I told her the story of how I had policed the landing on the night when Jenny Everett had had too much to drink. Mabel Mosscrop laughed emptily.

'You did your best, Mr Bailey. What time of night did you say this was?'

'Not long after you'd all come to bed. Some time between midnight and one.'

She laughed again, even more mirthlessly.

'I was up at half-past six, myself. Not on a law and order patrol. But just in time to see him coming out of her bedroom. I'm ashamed to say that I was the one who hid in the shadows. You say you'd heard her lock her door?'

'Yes. I'd stood still for a second on the landing, waiting for just that.'

'Well, he hadn't broken in. So she must have turned the key of her own accord.'

It did not make me feel sick, though it struck me that that was how I ought to have been feeling. But it emptied me of spirit. None of us who had anything to do with Miriam were really under any illusions about her. But we were all slightly touched with Mabel Mosscrop's brand of tragic optimism. We did have the habit of trying to weave delusions for ourselves out of such tatters as Miriam left us. We always had hope for Miriam—or liked to think we had.

Suddenly Mabel Mosscrop changed her tone. She became both quieter and yet more urgent. 'And I know what Police Inspector Brunt was getting at, Mr Bailey, underneath that hearty beer-swilling that he was treating us to. But Sam was too dense to see through it. How far had Sam ever gone with Miriam? That was what Thomas Brunt was prying for.'

I waited for her to answer the crucial question herself and she did so at once, without ambivalence.

'Sam Critchlow never let his thoughts stray in that direction for a moment, Mr Bailey. There was never any question on that score. He knew he'd never have set foot in this hotel again.'

Mabel Mosscrop had at least one quality that may not be common amongst Amazons: she was predictable. And Sam Critchlow knew which side his bread was buttered. When Mabel Mosscrop started behaving theatrically, it was rarely out of insincerity; it was purely out of emphasis. Now she became shrewdly confidential, showed a trace of almost girlish fear and actually gripped my wrist in her strong fingers for a couple of seconds.

'Mr Bailey, keep an eye for us on the way the wind is blowing. You have access to places where the rest of us daren't ask questions. Don't let them creep up on us. All we've ever done under this roof is an honest job.'

CHAPTER TEN

Walking back up the steep Bank to my house in the upper quarters of the town, the street lamps already extinguished, I tried again, very hard, to turn my mind from the present to the past. It was my only hope of obliterating the torture, to throw my thoughts back to the years when all seemed clean and all issues simple.

It seemed so now more strongly than ever. The newest revelation about Miriam had not shattered me. It was too logical for that, too inevitably the last scroll in the pattern. In fact, we had all in our various ways loved Miriam; and she had let some love her, without a thought for the effect she might be having on some men's minds. That was the ultimate simplification of it.

But how did Mabel Mosscrop think that I was going to keep any sort of track of the mental workings of Police Inspector Brunt?

In the event, the answer was served to me in such a way as to turn it into a very minor problem. As I let myself in at my gate, I was aware of a waiting presence in my front garden. I stood and tried to look about myself in the darkness; and the presence moved towards me out of the shadows. I smelled his waterproof coat—an article of apparel more suitable for a coachman on his box, that had been soaked times immemorial under rain and snow, and dried about his shoulders in the Peakland winds. Even the atmosphere in the *Little Rose* now bore its memories of that damp cloth.

'Mr Bailey, I have no right to be importuning you. It is late, and you have every right to be in your bed. But if I could have half-an-hour of your time?'

I hesitated; not because I had any intention of trying to send him away: nothing so undiplomatic. But I had remembered that my fire was out, the house cold, my study virtually undusted. He began almost to plead.

'It is because at this juncture, Mr Bailey, there are so many issues unresolved at one and the same time.'

'Of course,' I said, and apologetically preceded him through the front door whilst I lit the wall-bracket in the hall. The hissing flame, with its familiar stale smell, threw shadows over my hall-stand, my rack of walking-sticks and umbrellas and a lithograph of eighteenth century Mantua that had ceased to mean anything to me. I was aware of the shabbiness into which I had allowed my household to lapse, but resisted the temptation to apologise for it. My charity towards my ageing man-servant was greater than my consideration for myself, but I could hardly say that to Police Inspector Brunt. I spent, in fact, very little time in my own home these days and that mainly between bedroom, study and breakfast room. But I did not have to explain my personal dispositions to a policeman.

I took him into my study and went and fetched the patent oil heating stove from the glory-hole under the stairs. Mercifully its reservoir was still half full—I would not have known for certain where to look for paraffin. The Inspector kept on his outdoor coat. Even in the paltry heat that was coming from the stove, his cuffs and shoulders appeared to be steaming.

'It was principally—or at least amongst other things—about this character Critchlow that I wanted to talk to you.'

'I can't claim to know more about him than you must have seen for yourself.'

'He has quite a wit, though like the wagons he uncouples, it might be said to run along visible rails.'

'Quite.'

The policeman was not at the moment punctuating his speech with histrionic delays. He was talking in apparently natural tones, as might one professional man to another with whom he is in temporary and uneasy alliance. But I did not try to tell myself that this was the true Inspector Brunt. I was by no means convinced that any such creature existed.

'How long has he been frequenting the *Little Rose*?'

'I could not say,' I told him. 'Longer than I have.'

He brought out a vast, crumpled and grey handkerchief, and unexpectedly trumpeted into it for some seconds like a querulous rogue elephant.

'So it would be true to say that he had watched the Bennett girl grow out of her leggy childhood?'

'That would be true.'

'And his relationship with her always remained different from that with any other young woman he might have encountered in the place?'

'I cannot say about that.'

'Oh, come, Mr Bailey, are you not what the French call a *moraliste*? A student of human nature?'

Who was he to know what the French called their literary favourites?

'I like to observe people.'

'Well, then . . .'

I suddenly remembered a story. Miriam had been about sixteen at the time; before I knew her or of her. She had had a free afternoon once a week, and Mabel Mosscrop always saw to it that she made the long walk up to the hamlet beyond Fairfield, where her parents lived in bickering and squalor. Always she took with her a basket of left-overs from the hotel kitchen: a bone-end of ham, a bread-and-butter pudding, a dish or two or brawn scraps and a slice or two of cake. It was not a pilgrimage that she made enthusiastically, and as the years passed she dawdled more and more slowly past the shop windows of Spring Gardens.

But on her return journey, she always took a short cut by a row of cottages in a brook-bottom slum known as Hogshaw, and thence by a cinder-path that ran parallel to the railway goods yard and so into the town centre through the forecourt of the station.

To do this she had to run the gauntlet of a knot of raucous and impoverished housewives, who spent most of their time reinforcing each other's philosophy over yard walls. She was known to them by name—and also by supposed reputation—as something of a traitor to their class, who was giving herself airs, albeit still juvenile ones, in a hostelry which was already suspect amongst those who did not use it.

These women used to cat-call her and Miriam had neither the common sense nor the self-control not to answer them back. On one particular afternoon, one of her witticisms brought a clod of earth thumping into the back of her neck. She stooped to throw it back. And although she was not aiming at any particular target, she was unfortunate enough to draw a trickle of blood from one of the many runny-nosed offspring of Hogshaw. Thereupon she was set upon *en masse* by the enraged women, and was lacerated, bleeding, and fearful of having not a stitch left on her back when the attack was called off with a suddenness that suggested the arrival of unchallengeable reinforcements.

She looked and saw that it was Sam Critchlow, coming out of the kissing-stile of the goods yard with his rolling nautical gait and carrying his shunting-pole at the high port in his right hand.

The harridans retreated in a single cringing wave. It was futile to speculate on what was the actual effect that Critchlow had on these women; but it was a mob reaction, and evinced no kind of doubt. Sam Critchlow walked back with Miriam along the cinder-path and personally delivered her at the Rose.

Inspector Brunt listened faithfully, but did not take down any written notes. But when I had finished, he nodded, as if he did in fact set some deeper value on the tale.

'In fact, you might say that he was almost as concerned for Miriam Bennett, as child and as woman, as if he had been her acknowledged natural father?'

This caught me as might a blast of north-easter on the flank of Mam Tor.

'But, Inspector Brunt, I know of no reason to suppose...'

'Nor do I, Mr Bailey. No reason whatsoever. Except a certain common colour in events.'

He folded a corner of the grubby handkerchief and dabbed at the moist film that obscured his vision.

'In fact, Mr Bailey, the point arrives at which we are forced to admit that Miriam Bennett–Miriam Bonsall was no more than a common prostitute.'

I was forced to signify that I had to agree, though but for what Mabel Mosscrop had told me about the night of Roger Weigall, I might, even at this late stage, have attempted some kind of spirited denial. At any rate, I did my best to qualify the image.

'At least—an uncommon one.'

'You mean that that was what every client liked to think of her. But how uncommon is that?'

'I was never her client,' I hastened to assert.

'Of course not. But looking back at her history in this light, you might find an interesting thread through the tapestry.'

'Such as what?'

'Such as that each and every one of her courtiers—or almost each and every one of them—thought of himself as the one who might rescue her from the Rose.'

'Possibly.' I shrugged it off. I no longer felt personally involved.

'You never harboured any thoughts yourself—you'll forgive my asking this, sir, but the records must have no gaps in them—you never thought of yourself as a rescuer?'

I smiled; and I dare say I looked a little rueful.

'I hardly considered myself a match for the competition. I certainly never chanced my arm. If the thought ever entered my head, I pushed it firmly out again. You called me a *moraliste* just now; it would be more appropriate to think of me as an idle dreamer: a man too easily satisfied by the images he conjures out of air. She was a pleasant woman to see in the background. It would have been a good deal less pleasant if some of us had known for certain what she was really up to.'

'Or was it that you did know, and didn't want to face up to it?'

'Let's get back,' I said, 'to what we were originally talking about. Did I ever think of myself as a knight errant? The answer is further no; in my case it would certainly never have worked. Any more than it would have worked in the case of Andrew Wilson.'

Inspector Brunt now did pause—to refresh himself from his notebook.

'Now that is another character that I need to know more about. Likewise his nephew, the historian. And Stephen Stanhope—'

'With Stephen Stanhope there was nothing sordid. That was pure knight errant.'

Inspector Brunt accepted my assurance vacantly. 'Certainly,' he said, 'I am inclining ever more to your view that old Jonathan Bonsall did no more than pick the weapon up. And if that is the case, the prosecutor's office will not thank me for taking longer than I need in starting them off on a fresh brief.'

'It certainly seems curious that so many men from the past should have happened on the scene.'

'Not curious to me at all.'

He seemed unusually categorical; and familiar almost to the point of proffering friendship.

'Perhaps it was because she had sent for them,' he suggested.

CHAPTER ELEVEN

Perhaps I owe it to myself to spend more of my time writing. It is a relief to take up my pen and transport my mind back to the decent days.

That afternoon when I thought I knew that Jonathan Bonsall was hiding over the lip of Sawyer's Moss, the rest of the General's party was aware of nothing—there was not one of them who had a real eye for a stretch of country. We returned to the Hall, and it was a long time before I was about to break away from their company; there was a long and futile council of war, in which the General advanced plans for a strip by strip search of his land that could not have been achieved without the recruitment of a private army.

It was late in the evening before I got away, and I went straight to the spot where I guessed Jonathan to be: a small millstone quarry that had been abandoned years ago, after yielding enough stone for a few hundred yards of wall and an arc of shooting-butts.

He was making no attempt to conceal himself. The young rogue must have been watching my progress up the hillside long before I came upon him. He knew that it was me, and he had no fear whatever that I might betray him. He had fashioned himself a crude rock shelter from loose boulders and was protected from nocturnal draughts and rain less than torrential. He had cleared loose stones away from the space he had chosen for his bed, strewn the area with heather branches and laid down his blankets. He had lit himself a small fire, and I noticed that he had collected a small store of brushwood for future kindling.

As I came up he was sitting on his pallet, confidently cheerful, a tight black peaked cap on his head, and in his hand a small clay pipe, in which he was smoking his last plug of twist for the day.

I made myself angry with him. What he was doing was so senseless, so dangerous, so foolhardy and so inconsiderate of a young woman who deserved better treatment.

'What the hell do you think you're playing at?'

I noticed that he had his old suitcase half hidden under a pile of rubble, and a battered fisherman's creel that had played its part in both our lives. It was now lying open to display his store of cheese, bread, bacon and hard tack biscuits.

He jumped to his feet and kicked in a burning branch that had wandered from the edge of his fire.

'I'll show you what I'm playing at.'

He did not ask me to come with him, but knew that I would follow him down the hill. He dropped down from ridge to ridge with practised heels and I was at some points as far as thirty yards behind him. Finally we came down to level ground and he stood and waited for me. We walked a little further without speaking, and then he stopped and pointed to the eaves and mock Tudor chimneys of a folly cottage at the other side of a broad clearing. MacTaggart's: the mid-nineteenth century in all its affluence, doing its best to imitate the sixteenth in its poverty: half-timbering, and lime-washed plaster, perfunctory tracery in the woodwork, poky mullioned windows where daylight could so easily have been afforded, and a porch that aped a lych-gate. Architecturally a horror that defies descriptive justice, but it held a great appeal for the age that had built it. And Jonathan was understandably fooled.

'I'll show you what I'm playing at. That's where I'm going to live.'

'Meaning to live there, are you? The only home you're

'Behind the wall, beneath the trees,
They took their man by moon's first glow;
And as he sank to suppliant knees,
The lady to the tower did go—'

'Right! To the river with him!'

But they did not succeed in getting him to the water's edge. A voice called angrily from a distance; Jonty could not see who it was.

'One—two—three—'

They swung him backwards and forwards and then let him go, over the edge of the lawn into the soft earth of a flower-bed. He started to push himself to his feet and saw them running off. The girl was with them, and seemed to be laughing as hilariously as they were.

The park keeper came up as he was dusting the soil from his sleeves and trouser-legs.

'Well, by God! It's Jonathan Bonsall's lad. Fine-feathered company you're keeping tonight, young friend. Bloody young heathens.'

'I thought they were tormenting that lass.'

'Tormenting her? Miriam Bennett? She wants tormenting, that one does. She could have showed *them* the way out of the puzzle garden, if she'd wanted to. I wouldn't risk my shins to get her out of a dragon's cave.'

Jonty examined the damage. His jacket pocket was torn away in a great triangular rent. There was soil inside his shoes and down his collar. He had to go back to the maze to retrieve his walking stick, and its varnish had been badly grazed.

He could not go home yet in this state. If he entered the house before his mother had gone to bed, there would have to be explanations that he was too weary to want to make. Nor did he want to arouse the curiosity of the brothers with whom he shared a bed. He walked up in the direction of the ballroom, some of whose great glass doors were open against the sultriness of the night. He found a bench on one of the terraces, well away from the publicity of the nearest lamp-standard, and sat there for a long time idly watching couples coming and going in the fresh air between dances. And he caught sight of one of the young men with whom he had fought—a well-built but chinless character, with square-cut sideboards and a lot of hair. Miriam Bennett was with him: they stood together on the outer edge of the dancing-floor, looking out into the darkened gardens and eating some kind of sweetmeat out of glass goblets.

Jonty had not paid much attention to the park keeper's opinion of Miriam: he had, in fact, barely heard his words. He felt now indescribably sorry for himself: the sight of her in the company of another man seemed to suggest that she was lost to him for ever. Yet there was a mis-understanding that had to be put right. She would not, he felt sure, have laughed at him if she had known why he had acted as he did. In a way, he felt that she owed him an apology; and yet he owed it to himself to make her an explanation. It was beyond his understanding that any lady in difficulty should not want to be rescued.

The orchestra struck up again, with the sweet and satis-fying initial rasp of violin bows across strings. Music, of any kind in any setting, was always a special experience for Jonty. The Alexandra Quadrilles: couples who were taking the air quickened their steps to get back on the floor. Jonty picked up a morsel of gravel from the path and flicked it idly into the leaves of a plant in front of him.

The next morning, amongst the other clerks, he tried to find out if anyone knew anything about Miriam Ben-nett. So casually, so obliquely and affecting such in-difference that the true reasons for his interest were plain to everyone.

'Aiming high, then, are we, Jonty?'

'High?'

His face betrayed the second-to-second rise and fall in his spirits.

'No, that isn't what I mean. Not high. But from what I've heard, she knows how to enjoy herself, does Miriam. I think you'll find her tastes a bit expensive.'

'I wasn't thinking of spending any money on her.'

The opportunity ever to do so seemed barely credible. The other looked at him without belief.

'No?'

It was a blow to Jonty to learn that she worked as a barmaid. Perhaps that might be something else to rescue her from.

'Well, that's what she is, when all's said and done. But she's a bit more than that, really, as far as the *Little Rose* is concerned.'

Jonty had never met a barmaid before. Every element in his upbringing from the hearth rug scripture lessons of infancy, had dwelled on the evils of the bottle. And of all the inns in the town, the *Little Rose* was the last in which he had ever pictured himself taking an interest. He had always accepted that it was rather a specialised sort of place, though he had never bothered to work out in his mind in what sense he thought so.

That evening, he walked several times up and down before its frosted door before he went in.

CHAPTER FOURTEEN

The interior of the Rose surprised him. The mingled smells caught his throat: stale beer, sherry stored in the wood, and laminated tobacco smoke. He had expected a den of evil, but had never really considered what he thought the trappings of evil were: certainly an image of transparent shabbiness. Instead, he found himself in a setting more luxurious to his eyes than any in which he had ever set foot in his life: flashiness was not amongst his concepts. Red plush seats, marble-topped tables, rococo ironwork, a multiplicity of mirrors: he had seen nothing like it except on the stage at the Opera House.

I was in my usual corner, waiting for my usual friends to arrive. He did not look at me, and I was glad of that, for I knew that the sight of an old family friend would have embarrassed him. He saw Miriam at once. She was at the far end of the bar, Sam Critchlow's corner though Sam was not there at the moment, talking to two men who were only occasional callers. She finished what she was saying to them before she paid any attention to Jonty. He stood, a little nervously, at a vacant space near the beer-handles, and she turned presently and came towards him.

'Oh, hullo.'

'Hullo,' he said.

She was wearing a black dress, an austerity that she did not often seek, but which set off her charm, I think, more than she ever imagined. He stood looking directly at the disconcerting curve of her bosom. Her hair was less intricate than she had worn it for the ball, but red as a cello under soft lamp-light. She smiled at him: a glorious smile.

I felt for him. I knew what it was like to have one's innermost secrets melted. And her teeth were gorgeously white, one of them just the tiniest shade crooked.

'What can I get you?'

'I'd like a ginger wine, please.'

That was a compromise with his principles: the sort of thing that could respectably be asked for by those who did not normally take strong drink at all. She poured it for him, a large one, in a kind of glass that he had never handled before: tall, narrow-waisted and so full to the brim that he did not know how he was going to set about picking it up.

She returned with his change, and I could see that he was schooling himself to say something to her. But as soon as she had put the money into his hand, she went back to the two men. Jonty sipped his drink, rested one elbow on the bar and began to look round him at leisure. There were bottles with evocative labels from romantic corners of Europe. There were flagons of port, decanters of spirits, racked wine in dark green bottles. Perhaps he was wondering what impelled men to spend so much of their time here. I followed his eyes and began to ask myself the same question. There was no evidence of intemperance in sight, nothing to suggest the vices that filled the abstentionists' tracts, no suggestion of broken homes and abused wives and children.

The two men talking to Miriam Bennett were not even touching their glasses, which stood some inches from the fingers on the bar, as if they had forgotten them. Odds and ends of their conversation drifted over to Jonty, and it was veering towards vulgarity, but harmless enough—though Jonty probably did not think so. Miriam was laughing most of the time, an affected delicate tinkle, that broke down occasionally into a common guffaw.

The men were teasing her and she was enjoying it. They were making outrageously unfunny remarks about articles of clothing such as trousers, and being unable to sit down after a long bicycle ride.

Jonty began to look systematically about the less immediate corners of the room: at the hunting-field prints on the wall, at a row of toby jugs on a shelf slightly askew over a door. In a corner, up against the wall, stood an upright piano, one of its pedals broken, its front panel covered by a green pleated curtain. Jonty looked at it uncertainly, then visibly made up his mind. He took a step towards the group, hoping that the mere fact of his movement would attract Miriam's attention.

But she did not look in his direction, was too engrossed in a story one of the men was telling.

'Miss . . .' Jonty said.

She half inclined her head towards him, and without really looking at him reached out with one arm behind her for the ginger wine bottle.

'No, thank you, I don't want another one—not just yet.'

'What, then?'

'Out across the yard and it's the second door on the left,' one of the men said, and all three of them roared with laughter.

'No. I mean the piano.'

'What's the matter with it?'

'Is it there for anybody to play?'

'Don't tell me *you* can.'

'A bit.'

'Help yourself,' Miriam said.

Jonty Bonsall's piano playing was something I had heard about from his father, but which I still had to hear for myself. And, of course, I had my reservations about the stories Jonathan told. From the earliest age, it seemed, Jonty had shown virtuosity on any musical instrument that fell into his hands, whether it were a penny whistle, a child's toy dulcimer, an auto-harp or a concertina. He had a sure ear and a true sense of pitch. Once he had a melody in his brain, his fingers found the way to pick it out. Jonathan had lost no time in introducing him into one of the houses at which he worked, during the absence of the owner, and had sat him down at the piano keyboard. After a preliminary exploration of black and white keys, he had played 'Till we meet on that beautiful shore' from beginning to end. There was an instrument in the vestry of his chapel, and he sat in there for hours alone in the evening, though not without stirring up some elderly discontent at the secularity of some of the pieces that he taught himself. All was grist to Jonty's musical mill.

I had never heard him play. It was not, I must confess, an experience for which I yearned. But in common with several other people in the *Little Rose* that evening, I was in for a surprise.

Jonty went over and lifted the lid. At either end of the keyboard there were rings made by the bottoms of wet glasses. The keys were yellowed with age, gnawed by tobacco burns, worn and pitted, their edges rounded from unkindly pounding. The instrument was badly out of tune. The first chord that he struck came obviously as a shock to Jonty. The action was stiff, the response sluggish. The keys were shallower than those at the Wesleyan chapel.

But after a few slips at first, Jonty gave a good account of himself—by the standards of his present audience, a brilliant one. He played 'Over the Waves' and a set of improvised variations to 'Home, Sweet Home'. He played the 'Tinker Polka' and the 'Stephanie Gavotte'. He had a strong sense of rhythm and a phenomenal musical memory. His harmonies were elementary but adequate.

Whilst he was playing, the bar filled up. It was the beginning of that hour which was popular with most of the *Little Rose*'s friends. He had to play against a countercurrent of conversation, which he ignored. Someone asked for 'Beautiful Ohio' and he obliged.

And there was the pressure of a woman's bosom over

135

his shoulder, an intoxicating wave of feminine scent. Miriam Bennett was leaning over him, bearing on a tray another schooner of ginger wine, with the compliments of Mabel Mosscrop. Miriam smiled another of her special smiles for him, not intended to be shared with anybody else.

'Hey,' she said. 'You know, you're not bad.'

CHAPTER FIFTEEN

Inspector Brunt called on me in my office. I had gone in at about ten o'clock and had an appointment at eleven.

Every time I had met the man, he had contrived to present himself in a different light, and today he appeared in yet a new guise. Only the shabbiness of his appearance, little short of offensive, remained the same; was there a household of hungry and demanding little Brunts tucked away somewhere, so that his own clothing was nothing more than a regrettable necessity, to which he attended only at the fag-end of his meagre stipend? And yet today even his vision appeared to be less blurred than usual. His manner was brisk, business-like, almost professionally confiding, leaving me to wonder whether the real reason for his visit were something other than it purported to be; for there is a certain type of policeman from whom apparent overtures of friendship are not to be trusted.

He sat with his long coachman's coat unbuttoned—having declined the invitation to take it off—and made a play of coming straight to the point.

'The more I think about it, the more curious it seems to me that a courtship culminating in marriage should have taken place between Jonty Bonsall and Miriam Bennett.'

'It didn't surprise me,' I said. 'They had their set-backs, but the course of their relationship was fairly predictable.'

'You'll understand, Mr Bailey, that I am looking at everything all along the line. The tap-roots of what eventually happened must clearly be traced underground: a long way underground. And those two appear to me to have been an ill-assorted couple.'

137

'From Bonsall's point of view, Inspector, I don't think there's any cause for surprise. She bowled him over like a solitary nine-pin.'

'You approved of the match, did you?'

Both the content and the tone of the question took me by surprise. I laughed a little.

'Why should I approve or disapprove?'

'You took a close interest in both parties.'

'True. But not to the extent of wishing to interfere in either of their lives.'

Brunt paused. I thought for an instant that he was going to revert to his former habit of interspersing his talk with wearying silences; but he resumed before too long.

'I would prefer a plainer answer than that to my question, Mr Bailey.'

I considered myself rebuked, but very mildly. His manner was extremely polite this morning.

'All right, since you have me in the witness-box, you can say that I approved. I am essentially an optimist. I appreciated that there might be difficulties; but if things went right with them, the match was the best thing that could happen to both of them.'

'And how would you characterise their difficulties?'

'The princess and the puritan: not blood royal you understand, but she had had more than a taste of the pleasures that belonged to sophisticated society, compared with anything that Jonty had ever known. And he came from stock on both sides that set a premium on personal discipline for its own sake.'

'Old Jonathan a disciplinarian?'

'In his demands from everyone except himself.'

'Ah. So you thought that she would widen Jonty's horizons? And that he would make her want to match his ideals?'

'If she loved him.'

'Ah,' he said a second time. 'And that is what worries me.

It isn't as if there wasn't plenty of competition in the field.'

'No.'

'So how did Jonty set about it? I would have thought that she would have found him a little on the comic side.'

'Perhaps she did at first.'

I remembered enjoying, in the early stages, some very droll conversations between Miriam, Mabel Mosscrop and Sam Critchlow, Miriam reporting Jonty's clumsiness as if he had been one of Shakespeare's clot-polls.

'But he wasn't bad-looking, you know. He was energetic. He had a witty tongue. And she must have been at least slightly tickled by his attentions. Then there was his piano playing: he could give her anything on the keyboard that she asked for—and she was very much attached to senti-mental ditties. So it wasn't as if everything was loaded against him. Though when he suggested taking her for a walk in Grin Low Woods...'

Inspector Brunt came near to chuckling. 'He took Miriam Bennett for a walk in Grin Low Woods?'

'She was anything but keen at first. It was two or three years now since Miriam Bennett had walked further than the shops or the Pavilion. Since her mother had died, her weekly walks to Fairfield had come to an end. She didn't traipse up with cold bread-and-butter pudding for her father. She hadn't a pair of shoes that were suited to tramping over tree roots and sharp stones. And she dressed for the outing as if it were a fashion-parade along Broad Walk that she was attending. I watched them set out. She looked positively flimsy—diaphanous: whereas, in point of fact, she was neither. And in the *Little Rose* that even-ing, she was absolutely limping about; though she had the good humour to exaggerate, and make a joke of it.'

I remembered that evening well. We had all joined in the banter. There is an old saw about the world loving lovers and we made a lot of good-natured assumptions about the couple that probably did a lot to help Jonty Bonsall on his way.

'All of you?'

Inspector Brunt's question was sharp and astringent.

'I'm not saying that we were working hard to encourage them. All I am talking about is idle bar chatter.'

'Sam Critchlow? Did he encourage them?'

'No. Emphatically, he didn't. He didn't like even the most amiable jokes that we others were making about it. I don't think I ever have seen him so single-minded about anything. He said that he liked both of them too much to see them ruining each other's lives.'

'And Mrs Mosscrop? Whose side was she on?'

'Mrs Mosscrop? At this stage, anyway, she was on the side of the *Little Rose*. She was certainly responsible for Miriam not turning down that Sunday afternoon walk. Mind you, I'm not saying that she was looking to the couple's future. But the Mosscrops had taken on Jonty two nights a week as bar pianist. More's the pity: that was another six hours a week of peace lost. But none of us grudged the Mosscrops a roomful of paying customers.'

'Stop a minute. Bar pianist. That's a rum job for a puritan.'

'It was harmless. Quite a different sort of light used to come into Jonty's eyes when he flexed his fingers over a keyboard. Even if he was only going to rehash the Alexandra Quadrilles.'

'And what did his mother—and his chapel—have to say about it?'

'Alice Bonsall was uneasy, as you can imagine. But what would you expect her to do about it? Jonty was earning three times as much a week on that piano as he was in the Town Hall and nine-tenths of it was going into the household. What would you expect even Alice Bonsall to do with her husband in South Africa? Besides...' I hesitated.

I was unconvinced of the true depth of Brunt's sensibility.

'Besides, Mr Bailey?'

'She trusted him. She was that sort of mother and he was that sort of young man.'

Brunt nodded. I felt in that moment that somewhere behind his sordid daily round, beneath the squalid neglect of his appearance, the Inspector was somehow in touch with emotional reality.

'To come back to Mrs Mosscrop...'

'Her main concern at first was to see that Jonty wasn't offended. As a little example: while Jonty and Miriam were in the woods, he had picked her a bunch of wild flowers—wood anemones, trailing tormentil, burnt orchid. I'm afraid they didn't mean very much to her. They weren't the first blooms she'd been given in her life but all the others had been sent round from the florist's. These simply embarrassed her. She came home with them wilting in her hand, put them down just anywhere. It was Mabel Mosscrop who revived them in water and put them in a glass on a shelf behind the bar. In her way she was mothering Jonty, too.'

'I see. And what about Mosscrop himself? Did he never make advances to the girl?'

'Jack? As man to man, Inspector, any serious advances that Jack Mosscrop could make to anyone were atrophied in pickle many years ago. Even his own doctor says that he's defying medical science by remaining on this earth. Oh, he wasn't beyond slapping her bottom on the sly—in the most respectful way, if you can understand such a paradox. He used to lean nearer to her than he need, if they happened to be together behind the bar.'

'But she never found him offensive?'

'I don't think he bothered her. She probably hardly noticed. His wife certainly wasn't worried. She'd know better than anybody else, wouldn't she, what sort of a danger he would constitute? I don't think you fully appreciate, Inspector, just how thoroughly amiable and useless Jack Mosscrop is. They dress him up smartly once a year and keep him sober far enough into the day to renew his licence at the Brewster Sessions.'

'And the general opinion is that Sam Critchlow has his eye on that licence eventually?'

'Really, Inspector, I refuse to be drawn into compounding hearsay evidence.'

'And quite correct of you, Mr Bailey. If only all witnesses were as scrupulous. Mr Roger Weigall, now. How did he react to this young courtship?'

'As far as I can remember, he was not in the district at the time.'

'And Mr Andrew Wilson?'

'He came on the scene later. That is a separate story and one on which I would not care to embark except at leisure.'

I looked at my watch. 'And I have a client . . .'

'You will excuse me if I make a few notes, Mr Bailey? I shall not be more than a couple of minutes.'

He brought from an inside pocket a sheaf of papers, evidently torn in bulk from a notepad and folded once, unevenly, down the middle. He put them down on a corner of my desk, and quite frankly turning his shoulder to me, so that I could not see what he was writing, he turned some of them over and added notes here and there. When he had finished, he turned to face me again and smoothed down the top sheet with his stubby, scaly fingers. At the same time he gave me one of his infrequent smiles and looked me direct in the eye.

'One sheet for everyone I can think of who might possibly have committed this crime.'

'Rather a lot of them,' I said pleasantly.

'*Embarras de richesses*—but then I am applying some-what broad criteria—a policeman's terms of reference, rather than those of a poet or a *moraliste*. In my work, I have to be a realist. Possibility of access to the inn yard at the time of day in question, is what I am working on.'

His eyes remained on me, and I jumped to the conclusion that he wanted me to react.

'In that case...' I tried to insert a little laugh, but it sounded very artificial. 'You must have a sheet there for me, too.'

By way of answer he shuffled through the sheets of paper like a pack of cards and drew out one which he laid down on my blotter, the right way up for me to read. At the top my name was printed in capital letters and underlined; there was no other entry.

'As you can see, Mr Bailey, a virgin sheet. I make no apologies for treating you exactly as I am treating everyone else.'

'Of course.'

There was still the vestige of a smile on his face, and I hope that I reciprocated with good grace. The point that he was making was reasonable enough. But I found it disconcerting, nevertheless. I had the feeling that the whole underlying reason for his visit had been to establish this point and to leave me thinking uncomfortably about it. He gathered his notes together and returned them to some cache within his clothing.

'Did you take my advice, Mr Bailey, and start to compile a written record of your impressions of these events?'

His eyes had not appeared to stray in the direction of my quarter leather manuscript book, which was in fact lying closed on my desk, not far from my hand. I had already formed the habit of carrying it with me from my home to my office and back.

And I did not know now whether he had noticed it and was making one of those processes of felicitous induction beloved by the detectives of sensational fiction. Perhaps it was a shot at hazard.

'Yes,' I said. 'I am finding the task absorbing. One fact, as you suggested, has a way of calling forth another.'

'Quite so, Mr Bailey. I hope I shall be privileged to read your chronicle in its entirety. Or even individual episodes, as you complete them.'

'You will be very welcome to,' I said.

What other attitude could I have adopted? There was nothing incriminating in the document—and I certainly could not afford the luxury of appearing unco-operative.

Yet I hoped very keenly that he was not going to ask for the book here and now. There were some pages that I was very anxious to read over again before I allowed them to pass out of my hands.

For seconds he appeared to be hovering with the intention of asking for it. And then he must have dismissed the idea from his mind. He stood up and laboriously buttoned his coat. I noticed that the button that had been missing the other day had now been replaced; but by one which did not match its fellows.

I kept my client waiting unpardonably for five minutes. There were some pages that I did in fact read again immediately the Inspector had taken his leave.

CHAPTER SIXTEEN

In the days immediately following her walk with him in Grin Low Plantation, there was a perceptible cooling off in Miriam's attitude to Jonty. Superficially, we made jokes about her making sure not to let herself in for any more unwonted physical exercise. Deeper down, of course, most of us thought she was merely trying to stimulate him with a few pin-pricks of jealousy. It was her habit to keep her admirers lively in this way even if she had no serious interest in them. As far as being in or out of love with Jonty was concerned, I am quite sure that he was just another of the throng to her at this time. Deeper feelings came later. And I will defend Miriam before the bar of the hindsight cynics: her loving Jonty may have been short-lived—but while it lasted, she was consumed by it.

Jonty played the piano in the *Little Rose* on Wednesdays and Saturdays. We did not therefore expect to see him for two or three nights after he had picked her that bunch of flowers. But on the Monday evening he came in fairly early, in straw boater and carrying his walking stick, and drank a couple of schooners of ginger wine at the counter. This was in itself a new departure. Normally he sipped modestly at the glass or two that were brought to him at the piano; he showed no signs whatever of beginning to acquire a taste for what he was drinking.

Miriam served him casually. She was waiting at the same time on a group of young men which included some of those who had imprisoned her in the maze. But she had not previously shown much interest in this bunch, either. In fact, we were beginning to wonder whether she might be feeling a little out of sorts—until Jonty came in.

Then she moved within earshot of the young men's table and was very quickly involved in their characteristic chaff.

I felt sorry for Jonty. He was left alone standing at the bar, and I tried to signal to him to come over and join me. I would have enjoyed the opportunity to begin to get to know him. But Jonty was too miserable to want to be befriended by anyone. And when Miriam, having refilled his glass, turned her back on him again, he took himself out into the street without wishing us all more than a bare goodnight.

But things went better for him on the Wednesday, when our garish mirrors were once again vibrating to the 'Cuckoo Waltz' and 'Red Wing'. Sam Critchlow treated us to a spirited rendering of 'The Relief of Lucknow' and 'The Fox':

'Locks, bolts and bars shall fly asunder...'

Miriam carried Jonty's refreshment out to him during an interval between his pieces and perched herself sideways on a vacant chair and stayed talking to him. He must have been in that state of mind where he was hanging on every nuance in her deportment.

It was on this evening that plans were made known for a Saturday afternoon outing from the hotel for a picnic in Monsal Dale. These were the days when motor cars were beginning to appear on the roads, but there were many die-hards who did not believe that the horse would ever be supplanted; and some amongst them who were determined to do all they could, in their own little way, to ensure that this did not ever come to pass.

Consequently, the tour was to be made by wagonette— the char-à-banc of the pre-petrol era. And Miriam was to accompany the expedition. Mabel Mosscrop insisted on this. Substantial hampers were to be made up in the kitchen of the *Little Rose*, and so much of the hotel's crockery and glassware was at risk in wicker baskets under the back seat that it was considered prudent to have someone firmly reliable on hand to guard it.

It was Miriam who invited Jonty to go with them, extremely pressingly—not that he needed it. I do not know whether Mabel Mosscrop had persuaded her to do this. Perhaps some rumour had reached her of Jonty's dudgeon on the Monday evening.

It is at this point that Andrew Wilson comes into the story. During one of our later conversations, Inspector Brunt accused me of suppressing information about Andrew Wilson, or at least of reluctance to let my mind dwell on him. This I strenuously denied then, and equally forcibly refute now. Andrew Wilson played his part across the backcloth of Miriam's life for a relatively short while— between six weeks and three months at the outside. It was a vital part: one can say a decisive one. And presently I shall try to do proper justice to the facts. In the meanwhile, I could only have done the balance of my history an injustice by anticipating. I do not, like a police inspector, have to serve everything on the plate at once.

It was I who had persuaded Andrew Wilson to come to Buxton. At our Oxford college, where he was some ten years my senior, I had sat in his armchair, drunk his port and learned enough of Roman Law to satisfy the moderators. We were off-shoots of the same school, so he had taken an interest in me and forgiven me for—actually claimed to admire it—my constitutional laziness. Then he had surprised us by his marriage to a young lady of no scholastic pretensions, but exquisite tastes in the arts, and had left his college chambers to take up some appointment in Whitehall of which I know very little in detail but which brought him, if not fame, at least respect in influential quarters. Some five years before this visit to Derbyshire he was most pathetically widowed, and seemed likely to retreat into the morbidity of an anchorite: which was the main reason why I had urged him to come and see me up in the hills. I had not put him up in the *Little Rose*, thinking that he would prefer the anonymity of one of the larger establishments; and knowing that he could afford it. But I had coaxed him over to the Rose on one of our non-musical evenings, and to my surprise he took a liking to the place and started coming in often: a taste to which, I was presently to notice, the presence of Miriam contributed.

For some of his stay he had with him, as companions, his nephew Arnold Lowndes, a young reader in Modern History at Owen's College, and this young man's fiancée, a Miss Annabella Rossiter, an excessively intellectual young lady with an obsessive desire to involve herself in the transient feminist movement of the day.

Old Andrew was one of those men who had contrived to look middle-aged most of his adult life. He was now in his early seventies, not tall, but spare of frame and not running to an ounce of fat. There was no sign of infirmity in his gait, but all his movements were characterised by that deliberation which stems from dignity rather than sloth. In dress, as in the style of his language and bearing, he liked it to be felt that he belonged to the middle of the departed century rather than its end. Even to step the few yards from his hotel to the *Little Rose* he wore a black frock-coat, a silk top hat and wide trousers beautifully tailored to sweep the ground behind his heels, and yet rise graciously over his insteps.

He overheard the preparations that were being made for the excursion into the country and was astonishingly eager to have his party enrolled amongst the passengers. And when the Saturday dawned, and the party was being photographed in front of the inn prior to departure, it was patently obvious that Jonty was Miriam's preference for the day. It was Miriam who had reserved for him his place at her side in the much sought-after privacy of the back seat. It was Miriam who deftly, smiling but relentless, fobbed off the four or five others who had thought that they had a better claim to her favours.

The party was late in starting off. There were men whose feet were not so easily dislodged from the dented brass rail. And some of them were escorting young ladies in gossamer summer silks, not themselves buds of the *Little Rose*, who had to be waited for with worldly tolerance. But at last, with a crack of the long whip, they were careering down Spring Gardens, the variegated ribbons of the women's hats streaming behind them in the breeze. Miriam was sitting much more tightly wedged against Jonty than was actually necessitated by the number of people on their bench. She clung tightly to his arm as they swayed in overtaking a brewer's dray.

They tore down Ashwood Dale, flashed in a second past the gorge of Lovers' Leap, saw the river swirling through a scum of leaves and fallen twigs under the arches of the *Devonshire Arms*. Then they were swinging up Topley Pike, the girls screaming in exaggerated fear at the sight of the rocky valley deep below them.

Andrew Wilson's party were sitting on the bench in front of Miriam and Jonty. Bits and tags of conversation drifted back to the pair, and sounded like a sustained and bitter quarrel, for neither of them was accustomed to the notion of taking pleasure from scholastic dispute.

'And by *modern* you mean . . . ?'

'Post-Reformation.'

'Ah! Post-Reformation! The water-shed. Before which you no doubt suppose man to have wandered the arid plains in war-paint and with his club in his hand. I would have you know, young sir, that the administrators of our age face no problem that cannot be solved by reference to the Dialogues of Plato.'

'The administrators of the century preceding this appear to have overlooked the Platonic implications of not repealing the Corn Laws. Some of your Platonists were out-Platoed by the University Tests Act.'

'As pitiful an apologia as I ever heard.'

Down through Taddington Dale the bends on the road set axles and back-board creaking, seemed to threaten their vehicle with utter dismemberment at every new lurch. Jonty felt the warmth of Miriam's body, the trusting pressure of her fingers in his biceps.

They stopped for an hour in Bakewell and then took the upper road, over through the Longstones, stopping for their picnic in a broad meadow by the river in the shade of Monsal Head, near the arches of that rather handsome railway viaduct that occasioned such distress to the omniscient Mr Ruskin.

Miriam had to busy herself now, but there was no lack of hands eager to help her to lift down the baskets and deploy their contents. But even still, surrounded as she was by a swarm of men anxious to show their diligence, she managed to convey that her friend for the afternoon was Jonty. They sat together and ate from starched table napkins laid on the grass.

'And aren't you going to pick me any flowers today?' she asked him. 'I'll tell you what—you go and see what you can find. I've got to pack up now and keep my eyes open to see that we go back with everything we brought with us.'

He wandered up towards the railway embankment and picked some sheep's-bit scabious, a head or two of knapweed and meadow crane's-bill, and set the posy off with yarrow and yellow tufted loosestrife. When he returned, he could not see her at first. She was standing some distance away from the remainder of the group, talking to Arnold Lowndes. His fiancée had walked away and was standing with Andrew Wilson at the river's edge.

But Miriam swung round to welcome Jonty while he was still yards away from her.

'Oh, are those for me? You must look after them for me so that they aren't spoiled on the way home.'

They returned through Cressbrook and Litton, and up the long haul from Miller's Dale. Now it was Annabella Rossiter who appeared to be disputing fiercely.

'I would hardly expect you to be *directly* acquainted with the writings of Dr Pankhurst...'

'Upon my soul, young lady...'

Andrew Wilson was given to cultivating archaisms in his speech.

'Upon my soul, young lady: may I say that I have also read every word of John Stuart Mill, and am *au fait* with the views of Harriet Martineau, Mary Somerville and Josephine Butler. May I also add that my views more nearly coincide with that antagonism to your cause so ably expressed by Mrs Humphrey Ward, Mrs Creighton and Mrs Sidney Webb.'

There was a cool air in the evening. They trotted past Coningdale and Pig Tor into the gleam of the setting sun. Miriam leaned her cheek against Jonty's shoulder. But it was no use pleading fatigue when they arrived back at the inn. There was work to be done at once: the wagonette to be unloaded—and the willing hands that had manifested themselves in the meadow were no longer available, the party having dispersed as they jumped down on to the pavement. Miriam and Jonty had to do most of the immediate labour themselves, and then it was time for Miriam to change for the bar and for Jonty to claim his piano stool. For once, I was glad to see him back in office: a casual visitor was trying to pick out the Overture to Tannhäuser with his index-finger.

There were enough potential situations in the *Little Rose* within the next few days on which to found a Restoration Comedy. For a short while, I feared that Miriam was going to make a set at Arnold Lowndes. But the young historian made it plain that his loyalty to his oval-faced blue-stocking was unassailable. They were collaborating on some kind of radical pamphlet and thus, personal affection apart, were not to be tempted asunder. Consequently, thanks to a devious sequence of motives, Jonty was no longer the undivided light of Miriam's eye. He had to work for her attention and usually, but not invariably, won it. In retrospect, I rather fear that she was dangling him in front of her world as an object worthy of displacement. But this did not occur to me at the time, and the displacement, when it came, came from an unexpected source. And she did not descend to cold-shouldering Jonty the way she had done on that wretched Monday. She personally tended her vase of knapweed and sheep's-bit scabious until the petals dropped off.

I misread the effect she was having on Andrew Wilson at first. When first he edged me into a corner and started to talk about her charms, I simply thought he was under the same sort of remote and pleasant influence as many of us others were. He asked me questions about her age, her home, her background which I answered as informatively as I could. When he spoke as if he thought she had attended some young ladies' finishing school, I recognised the signs of a purblindness that was more advanced than I had expected. Where my answers—and my demeanour—did not satisfy him, he narrowed his eyes and embarked on a series of staccato supplementary questions. He seemed to think that he was still at his Civil Service desk and that I was some subordinate who was being unhelpful in an inquiry that might redound to my ultimate discredit.

It was from Mabel Mosscrop that I learned beyond doubt that his interest was running deeper than made sense. In that exaggeratedly secretive manner which she had when dealing with personal matters, she detained me in a corner one night when the company was thinning out and I was about to go home. Mabel Mosscrop is a very intelligent woman, but the quickness of her wits is only reliable when she is dealing with her familiar round. Outside her accustomed sphere she often shows herself quite lost; and she obviously found Andrew Wilson inscrutable. And this means, by a common system of thinking, that she was beginning to dislike him.

'Your friend is asking some pretty forward questions about Miriam.'

I rather resented the tone that seemed to hold me responsible for him, simply because I had introduced him into the place.

'He wants to take her out with his other two friends on Thursday afternoon.'

'I see no harm in that, if you can spare her.' I thought I had better add this rider. Mabel Mosscrop seemed to be in the mood to be easily upset.

'Oh, I can spare her. Till after tea. It rather looks as if I shall have to get used to the idea of sparing her, doesn't it?'

This was Mabel Mosscrop using ellipsis as her supreme dramatic device. I was slow, sometimes, to grasp the direction of her thought. I thought now that she had moved to some fresh angle, and was talking about someone else: perhaps even Jonty.

'Oh? Are there developments, then? Who . . .?'

'*Who?*' I thought she was actually going to become short-tempered with me. 'It's Mr Andrew Wilson that I'm talking about. Your friend.'

In all conscience, my affection for Andrew Wilson was beginning to wear thin. He was an older man than me and had allowed himself to appear to have grown older still. As a man on holiday he had more time on his hands than I had, which meant that I was not always beside myself with pleasure to see him. Professionally, he had behind him a familiarity with high places that I lacked and which he liked to keep as an unknown quantity from us all. Personally, he was wrapped up in a past about which he said nothing, but which I knew had been by no means as self-sufficient as he liked me to think.

'He is a very lonely man,' I said, conscious how lame this must sound.

'Apparently.' Mabel Mosscrop was not at pains to sound anything but acid.

Four or five years ago Andrew Wilson had lost a wife whom he idolised; though some of us had seen a bitter irony in the vision of how little some men are prepared to do for their idols. I remembered how once, in the prime of all our lives, we had caught up with each other on an overlapping loop of the Grand Tour, and risen to watch the sunrise on the Rigi Kulm. For three minutes Elvira and I had stood apart from the others, looking over an iron rail down into the rose-pink valley.

'I mean,' Mabel Mosscrop said, 'when it comes to asking me in a roundabout way how much compensation I would think fair...'

'Good heavens! You don't mean he's thinking of marrying her?'

'I don't know about that. But it's obvious he's thinking of taking her away from here.'

I thought to myself that the time was approaching when I would have to have a heart-to-heart talk with the young nephew. But I felt under no obligation to confide my tactics to Mabel Mosscrop.

'Well, I don't think any of us need worry over much,' I said. 'It's for Miriam to decide. And she's a woman with plenty of sense.'

But Mabel Mosscrop had only short shrift for my cheerfulness.

'Then I ask you: if Miriam Bennett had been left to her own decisions, where would she be now?'

I did not answer that. I do not know why it was, but there suddenly came into my mind the image of Jenny Everett.

CHAPTER SEVENTEEN

Miriam Bennett—Jenny Everett—and there were other names that Inspector Brunt had mentioned: Kitty Brindley and Annie Brightmore. What was I doing in this gallery? How had I become so committed to the *Little Rose*? For the space of two hours, on the evening when I had begun this chronicle, I had made some attempt to throw the shadow of the place off me. Yet here I still was. In vain did I try to tell myself that I was not the only one in my walk of life to whom the house had become a substitute for a gentlemen's club: the Borough Engineer and a don emeritus. I had wasted hours of my time in here, evening after evening, had not even allowed the jangle of Jonty Bonsall's hollow chords to drive me away.

There was another aspect of this business, to which I must start to apply myself with proper diligence. Whatever outcome Inspector Brunt might secretly be striving for (and I was by no means convinced that he had been honest with me about his motives) there were no signs yet of the withdrawal of the charges against Jonathan. Any day now I was expecting to see Jonathan's cause in the calendar, and that set me routine tasks that had to be as meticulously done as any involved in the transfer of a parcel of land. I had already received an operative promise from a barrister's managing clerk: I had settled on Mr Matthew Carey, who travelled the circuit. He was of no great eminence, but dogged and unyielding; I could have gone for someone more flamboyant. But I did not think that pyrotechnics in court were going to help us. As things stood on the file at the moment, the prosecution were not going to need any.

Carey would have to meet Jonathan, and by our professional usages, I would have to be present at the interview. But in advance of this confrontation, I paid another visit to Derby gaol myself. It was beginning to weigh on my conscience that there were certain details of setting and circumstance on which I had been contenting myself to rely too comfortably on second-hand accounts.

The inn yard, for example...

This time, I did not see Jonathan in his cell. He was brought to me in a small, bare room on the ground floor of the prison, with two hard benches and a scrubbed deal table. The warder who escorted him was a burly, silent man of unreadable opinions—if indeed he held any at all. Jonathan had lost his startled expression. His eyes were no longer wild with resentful surprise at being here. The grey rhythms of the place had settled on him. His shoulders sagged under his ill-fitting jacket. His walk had degenerated almost into a shuffle. This was a place where distances did not encourage any man to hurry and where most movement took place in frustrated files.

'I don't want to raise your hopes unfairly, Jonathan, but we do see a faint prick of light. There are some questions that I want to ask you.'

He had sat down uneasily on the outer corner of one of the benches. He had already reached the state of feeling uncertain of any action not performed as the result of a direct order. I must say that I preferred Jonathan Bonsall the outlaw.

The empty end of the seat suddenly levered itself into the air. The bench clattered on to its side, and Jonathan stooped to pick it up. I thought we might get a salutary laugh out of the incident; but Jonathan was suddenly angry to find himself subject to the laws of physical science. And I was grimly reminded of another sense in which the same principle was shortly going to be applied, unless our work bore more fruit than we had seen so far.

'Try and make yourself comfortable, Jonathan.'

He sat down properly, with his forearms on the table.

'I'm going to have to remind you about some not very pleasant things. About the inn yard...'

'I know. That policeman has been here, and he was talking about the same thing.'

I felt the fury storm up inside me.

'Brunt, he said his name was.'

'Listen, Jonathan, Inspector Brunt knows very well that I am representing you. He has no right whatever to talk to you at all, except in my presence.'

But Jonathan remained placid. He was utterly unaffected by this intolerable breach.

'He told me that. He said that I could refuse to talk to him, if I wanted to. The Governor's Assistant sat and listened to everything we said. And he told me the same thing.'

The Assistant Governor? The same one who had conducted the couple to the mortuary? I did not ask.

'Jonathan, if ever this happens again you must stand out for your rights. Inspector Brunt could be a very dangerous man.'

'I only told him the truth.'

'Perhaps.' I did not want to pursue this theme. I did not want to set Jonathan thinking in terms of constructive dishonesty. I did not want him telling lies; my inquiries were complicated enough as it was. But it was a question of presentation; and I preferred that Jonathan should be led, rather than briefed in advance.

'Inspector Brunt is on my side,' he said.

'He told you that?'

'I could see it for myself. He knows I didn't do it.'

Which only went to show how dangerous the man might be.

'You'd better try to remember all he asked you—and what answers you gave him.'

'It was mostly about the inn yard.'

'I know.'

'About how she was lying. Where her feet were and her head—what was left of it.'

He seemed unaffected by the gruesomeness of the memory, whereas I had been virtually apologising to him for re-introducing the subject. In fact, it was my own revulsion that I was afraid of. There was a feeling throughout the *Little Rose* now about the yard outside. I will swear that we men—except for the strangers, that is—were even going out to the urinal no more frequently than we needed. I cannot speak for how every individual felt; it was one of those subjects where one did not talk to others about what was going on inside one. For my own part, I could not be certain whether there was still a dark stain on the cobbles or not. Was I only projecting it, or interpreting a fleeting shadow? What shadows did Mabel Mosscrop see there? For she had been next on the scene after Jonathan. She still came and went through that back door, as domestic chores demanded. Was she still tormented by the memories of her pendulum relationship with the girl: the love and hate, the admiration and the jealousy, the swing between contempt and reliance on her, the moments of exasperation and the hours of dependence?

What of her husband? Was Jack aware of anything more than the departure of a familiar figure from the haze about him? Could he bear to see again the huddled angles of the walls round the space where it had happened?

What did Sam Critchlow think when he went out there? I was not impressed by Brunt's theory that he had been Miriam's father: but the fact was clear that he had a relationship with her that was not typical of the sort of man he liked us to suppose he was.

And what of those who had been only on the periphery of her existence? Arnold Lowndes and Roger Weigall, both

158

of whom had been on the premises at the instant of her death?

Yet could one, in the light of Mabel Mosscrop's revelation of the night of Jenny Everett, honestly describe Roger Weigall as being on the periphery of Miriam's existence?

Not unless one's attitudes to the relationships between people was a very nasty one indeed.

I forced my attention back to what Jonathan was saying.

'She was lying with her feet nearest to a tub of nasturtiums. Her skirt was rucked up about her legs.'

That was another thing. It had only been the day before that Jonty had died. Should not Miriam have been making at least some show of wearing mourning? I know that that would have been hypocritical, but that did not make it improbable. Wasn't that something that Mabel Mosscrop would have talked her into, even bullied her into, if only for the sake of respectable conventions and the precious reputation of her house? Wasn't the sentimental by-play of the shattered and remorseful widow just the act that Miriam would fancy, to lure her next victim?

But she had died in her everyday clothes. Was she inhumanly hard or merely trying to convince herself that she was?

'The axe was lying about four feet away from her on her left—well, *her* right. My left, where I was standing.'

I made ready to head him off. I would have lost my temper if he had said his usual thing about the axe. But he seemed to have worked this out of himself.

'So from the way she was lying, you think that at the moment she was attacked, she would have been facing you as you came out of the back door?'

'That's what I told the Inspector.'

'In other words, her attacker had come upon her from behind—from the direction of the sheds and stables?'

'He must have done.'

It seemed perfectly natural to me to be speaking of *her*

attacker. Hitherto I had believed in theory that Jonathan was innocent. Now I saw his innocence as a cold fact.

Though, of course, the prosecution could easily argue that he could have been poking about in the sheds, and himself have come upon Miriam from behind.

But, clearly, Inspector Brunt would have tested whether this theory could be eliminated.

'He seemed to think,' Jonathan said, 'that I'd been nosing about in the stables. He asked me where the Mosscrops had kept the axe. How the hell was I to know the answer to that?'

I hoped he had impressed the Inspector with the same tone of ingenuous self-assurance.

And I could have told him where the Mosscrops had kept the axe...

The day before I had finally marshalled my courage and slipped out of the bar in the evening to make a proper inspection of that yard. Perhaps *courage* is too conceited a word to use of a situation in which the only obstacles to be overcome were sententious and capricious. I had fought shy of this investigation, though knowing full well that it had to and would be done. At last I faced up to it.

And I, too, had come to the conclusion, supported by what I had been told about the manner in which her body had been lying, that Miriam had been struck from behind, very probably by an assailant who had been lurking in one of the sheds.

This opened up the possibility that she might have been killed by someone who had no immediate connection with the *Little Rose* and its circle. The yard formed a hollow square based on the sculleries and still-rooms of the hotel itself, bounded on the left by the high yard wall of a neighbouring tailor's shop and on the right by a congeries of stabling and outhouses. Access to the rear was by a narrow lane that wound round a blind corner, under two flourishing elms, into the steep little road that ran up from the town centre to the railway station. This approach was used regularly by tradesmen, brewers' draymen—even by thirsty travellers who were too impatient to come round to the hotel bar by the longer walk to its front entrance.

So it was neither unusual nor particularly suspicious for a visitor to come into the yard that way. The lane did not exactly teem with people, but it was treated quite often as a thoroughfare. So if the murderer were some outsider, the police would have an almost impossible task trying to collate casual information about men who might have been seen coming and going under the elms at the operative time.

And what was the operative time? I am no expert in forensic science, though I do of course know where I can turn professionally for informed opinion. I am not even confident about some of the firm assertions that are all too often being made at the present time in our criminal courts. In the wake of our many imaginative and lurid story-tellers, it is not uncommon for a case to be made to turn on a wisp of dust or a nail-trimming. But in the matter of how long a recent corpse has been dead, there is substantial agreement on principles. I did not know what precise conclusions the police had reached in Miriam's case nor even how long it had been before her body had been brought to the forensic table. But the time of her death must have been shewn to have been close to Jonathan's arrival on the scene, otherwise there would have been no case for holding him at all.

How long had she been dead when Jonathan had found her? Ten minutes, half an hour, an hour? Such precision as that, in any case, would have been elusive. But a new importance now attached itself to the recent movements of those who were already in the inn when Jonathan arrived.

Someone who had been out into the yard shortly before he appeared?

Someone, perhaps, who had seen him coming, and was quick witted enough to see the chance to incriminate him?

I questioned Jonathan closely on the points that bore on this. 'Tell me again: who was in the bar when you entered from the street?'

'Sam Critchlow. And two gentlemen I didn't know.'

'Describe them to me.'

'There was one who looked as if he fancied himself. Curly hair, plastered down with oil, but a lot of grey in it. The sort of man who doesn't know he's past it.'

'Roger Weigall.'

'And a younger man, not unpleasant looking. The police detective told me he writes history books.'

'Arnold Lowndes. And who was actually serving behind the bar when you came in? Mrs Mosscrop?'

'No. There was nobody there when I pushed the door open. You would have thought they weren't interested in customers. Then Jack Mosscrop came in—along the passage from their living-room. He looked as if he'd just got up. His hands were shaking.'

'He isn't far off *delirium tremens*.'

'His jacket and his waistcoat were unbuttoned and his tie was round his neck but not tied—not even properly under his collar. He looked back over his shoulder and called to his wife to come. I was just going to tell him that there was no hurry I hadn't come to spend my money, and she appeared. But it wasn't to serve me that he'd called her. He wanted her to fasten his buttons and tie his tie for him.'

'Which she did?'

'In a very bad temper. She was really rough with him. She did the buttons and the tie, but she looked as if she was going to shake him as you would a youngster. And

I can't say I blame her for that. When a man gets to the state of not being able to do jobs like that for himself...'

'Yes. You didn't see anyone else go into, or come from the yard?'

'No one at all.'

'Sam Critchlow didn't move from the bar?'

'Not an inch.'

'And the other two gentlemen?'

'They just sat quietly.'

'Together?'

'On the same seat. They seemed to be friends. They were drinking together.'

Which struck me as odd, or at least as interesting enough to be worth bearing in mind. Roger Weigall and Arnold Lowndes were not normally men who would want to spend long listening to each other. The only thing they had in common was that Miriam Bennett's shadow had fallen across their paths—in very different sets of circumstances.

Either of them, of course, could have stepped out of the back door for a minute during that crucial period, let us say half-an-hour, before the appearance of Jonathan Bonsall.

For that matter, Sam Critchlow might even have come into the Rose that way, his throat parched from a morning's shunting.

Much turned on how long these men had actually been here. And I had no doubt that Inspector Brunt had gone precisely into this. His resources for such inquests were much readier than mine; though I could see that I would have to make the effort.

And the more I thought about it, the more I thought that Sam Critchlow might repay closer study.

Yesterday, when I had finally faced reality, and gone out for my tour of the yard, I had done so in a spirit of second-to-second fear. I would be hard pressed to say exactly what I was afraid of—but the illogicality of it did not detract from its realness. I found myself stepping *over*, for example, the spot where Miriam had lain. That was not exactly fear, or at least not entirely fear, it was a sort of sentimental respect; but there was fear in it. It was the sort of evening—and the sort of setting—that brought echoes from a man's elemental inheritance. Dark had already fallen. There was light from some of the windows at the rear of the hotel, but this was tantalisingly dim, and not only did it hinder serious search—it receded into suggestive shadows. High up there I knew, unlit, was the garret window from which Miriam had often looked down, from the very earliest days of her entrance into the Rose as a shapeless slavey; not knowing that down there was the space where she would one day lie with her head stove in. It was absurd for me, an adult, an educated man, to allow myself to be disturbed by such a consideration. But it was a night for thoughts like these; and perhaps I had not yet had enough to drink.

Moreover I knew that not twenty yards from where I was sidling about in these shadows, there might exist a man who would have found my curiosity little to his taste. Sheer physical fear was not actually uppermost amongst my emotions, but it should logically have been so. The base of my skull was as vulnerable as Miriam's had been.

I pushed open the door of a shed and stumbled into a clutter of stored furniture: dismantled bedsteads, a chest of drawers, a bowl and ewer, a stack of framed pictures, including a nastily illuminated wall text: 'The Lord is my refuge and strength, a very present help in trouble'. I struck a match, and thought I could identify the spot where Jonathan had found and picked up the axe. I saw a horribly embossed brass pot that must surely be the *jardinière* that had caused so much distress. Obviously, when Miriam had left their cottage up on Burbage Edge, at the beginning of Jonty's prison sentence, their household effects were brought here by carrier. They were all here: broom, buckets, coal box and a towel rail. The axe would have been here too.

And if Jonathan had set foot in here, the first thing he would have gone to would have been the *jardinière*. He would at least have lifted it down.

The match went out between my fingers and I struck another, holding it at experimental angles to give myself the best field of vision and looking round for a lamp that I might light. But suddenly the door was snatched open, my match was extinguished by the draught, and my arms were pinioned to my sides by brutally uncompromising hands.

'One stupid move out of you, old friend, and I shall break your neck.'

Sam Critchlow.

'Steady, Sam. It's only me. Mr Bailey.'

Full marks to him for tackling a supposed burglar; but he seemed no less antagonistic when he discovered my identity.

'And what the hell do you think you're doing in here?'

'Pursuing essential inquiries.'

'And do you have the right to pursue your inquiries on private property?'

As far as the law was concerned it was a pertinent question, but he asked it as if it was his own property that he was defending. I did not like the way he pushed me out of the door. And he did not release my arms until he had me outside.

Mabel Mosscrop came out of the door of her scullery, leaving it open so that we were exposed in a scalene triangle of light.

'What's going on, Sam? Who is it?'

'Just another busy-body who thinks he's been promoted to police inspector.'

She saw who I was, and I expected her to say something

to tone him down. But she did not speak immediately.

'What I was looking for,' I said, 'was simply in the interests of justice.'

'It's a pity you can't leave well alone, Mr Bailey.'

'I told you several days ago: a man is entitled to his defence.'

'Then I suggest you work his defence out in your own office. You have no right whatever to be in that storeroom without my permission. You're a lawyer. You should know that.'

'I do. And I'm sorry.'

But she was clearly not disposed to consider the incident discharged by an apology. We stood and looked at each other, the three of us, without speaking. I knew in that moment that my *rapport* with the *Little Rose* was finished. I would never sit in that bar again. I had wasted God knows how many hours of my life in that atmosphere of stale smoke, stale liquor fumes and stale conversation. I turned on my heel and walked away from them, away from the trough of sickly light, passed the end of the shed in which the accumulation of the Bonsalls was piled, out up the slope of Station Approach.

And across the deal table of the prison ante-room, I felt sure that no policeman would have interrogated Jonathan Bonsall as badly as I was doing. I could not even save my mind from wandering.

'So,' I said. 'You then asked Mabel Mosscrop whether you might speak to Miriam Bennett. How did she react?'

'I didn't think she was going to let me. She didn't say anything at all at first. Just stood looking at me with her bottom lip working back and forth over her teeth.'

'She was afraid of you.'

'She had no reason to be. I was minding my manners.'

I was tempted to tell him that that alone ought to have had her on the *qui vive*.

'And then?'

'She said that Miriam was very upset, and had shut herself up in her room. She didn't think it would be a good idea to disturb her. I said that there had been one or two things on loan to Jonty that I wanted to have back. She said she would go and ask Miriam.'

'Which she did do?'

'She went through the door into their private quarters and I heard her go up the stairs.'

'What did you do then?'

'For a minute or two I just stood there. But you know me, Mr Bailey, never in my life have I had much truck with places like that. And I was determined not to put money into the Mosscrops' pockets. I went out—to relieve myself—I could have waited, but it helped to kill the time.'

'You didn't exchange any conversation at all with the other men?'

'They weren't the type to want to talk to me. That was one of the reasons I went outside.'

'I'd never thought of Sam Critchlow as stand-offish,' I said. 'Didn't *he* speak to you?'

'We weren't friends.'

He did not look as if he wanted to enlarge on this. When I pressed him, he said that the crux of their quarrel had been a long time ago. I told him that if I was to continue to help him, he would have to tell me everything.

'He took sides with Stanley Redfern,' he said.

'So you went through into the yard and the first thing that met your eyes...'

'I could see she was dead. She was in a terrible mess. The first thing I did was to pick up my axe. Because, I said to myself, somebody's killed her and they used my axe: the nerve of it. That was what upset me, Mr Bailey—the nerve of it.'

'And you just stood there looking at it?'

'Making sure it was mine.'

'And you *were* sure?'

'I'd burned my initials on the underside of the haft. But a man knows the feel of his own axe.'

'How long did you stand there?'

'I think I must have lost my proper sense of time. I wasn't frightened. I was disgusted. The thought never entered my head that they'd blame me for it. I was just going back into the house to tell them. Then Mabel Mosscrop came out.'

'But let's try to set a time to the interval: one minute, two minutes—five?'

'I don't know, Mr Bailey.'

He was helpless to help. The sight that would have made some men vomit and some men run had simply bemused him. Because of the nerve of it.

I rounded off the interview with a few empty phrases, ostensibly encouraging. The impassive, ram-rod warder stood by the open door. Jonathan rose meekly to be ushered back to his cell. Only after he had passed me along the metallically ringing corridor did he turn back with a crack in his voice.

'Mr Bailey, you'll have to get me out of here. I can't stand any more of it.'

A far cry from the slim figure in the tight black cap, smoking his twilight pipe on the hill overlooking MacTaggart's cottage.

CHAPTER EIGHTEEN

Andrew Wilson took Miriam for three outings altogether, and I was able to assemble the story from a representative series of angles: from old Andrew himself, because in his disingenuous way he tried to take me into his confidence and would perhaps have been more honest with me if I had offered him more encouragement. From Sam Critch-low, who gave some uninhibited twists to the story when we were out of hearing of the women. From Mabel Moss-crop and from Miriam herself. Both women made a point of stopping for conversation by a corner of my table at least once in the course of an evening. A civilised cour-tesy; my relationship with the Rose had never been better than at this particular time.

The first and shortest outing was to Poole's Cavern, one of the chartered Seven Wonders of the Peak. The posters proclaimed that the cave was so safe and spacious that the elderly and invalid could make the tour in their bath-chairs. But no mention was made on the placard of the water that dripped on hats and fur trimmings, or the thin film of liquid mud underfoot that was so inimical to Miriam Bennett's newest *glacé* kid shoes.

Incandescent gas lighting had been installed in a series of glowing yellow mantles that stretched for three quar-ters of a mile into the limestone hillside. In the concavities of the roof one could see where primeval waters had once swirled. Unnatural shadows stretched away into a darkness that suggested the eve of Creation. The place had a rough sort of beauty—Andrew Wilson was impressed. I had not dared to forecast whether he would be or not. He quoted Hardy to Miriam.

' "The new Vale of Tempe may be a gaunt waste in Thule: human souls may find themselves in closer and closer harmony with external things wearing a sombreness distasteful to our race when it was young." Egdon Heath. You've not perhaps yet read *The Return of the Native*?'

Miriam hadn't. In the last six weeks she had read fifteen pages of James Payn's *A Grape from a Thorn*, which for her was fair progress. Perhaps old Andrew's greatest weakness in courtship was his impatience to improve her. (Elvira had not been susceptible of improvement at his hands—but even with her he had never stopped trying.)

The party which they had joined reacted with delighted 'Ooh's' and 'Aah's' to the fanciful names which their guide gave to the various natural features: the 'Bee-hive'—a wave of stalagmitic deposit on a boulder; the huge stalactite known as the 'Flitch of Bacon'; the 'Fried Eggs'—globules of dripping lime that had taken on fresh colours from the mixing of mineral deposits. Then there was 'Mary Queen of Scots' Pillar', which marked the spot which the wretched woman had reached on her visit to the show place during her exile locally.

'And I don't blame her for that,' Miriam said.

'For what, my dear?'

Miriam was learning that Wilson's hearing was acute for his age. She really would have to curb her *sotto voce* comments.

'For turning back when she'd come as far as this.'

'Oh. I'm sorry. Aren't you enjoying yourself?'

'I'm cold,' she said. 'I'm getting wet. And it smells.'

There really was a disagreeable foulness in the air: a compound of dank lime, of unburnt gas, of visitors' damp overcoats and visitors' stagnant breath. Andrew Wilson sacrificed his interest in pre-history. They slipped away from the rest of the group and he brought her out into the warm, clean sunshine, holding her gallantly by the elbow. There was a smell of peat soil and leaf-mould in

170

the copse which surrounded the cave mouth.

In the foreground of the Cavern there was a collection of gauds for the entertainment of tourists whilst they awaited the guide. There was a so-called museum, containing a meretricious miscellany, a small bandstand and, in a large outdoor cage, an old and irascible monkey, who had ultimately to be got rid of since he scandalised so many visitors by sitting up against the bars, playing with his private parts. It required an effort on Miriam's part to get past this creature without bursting out laughing, and stern self-discipline from Andrew Wilson to pretend that he had not seen the cage at all (source of information, Sam Critchlow).

Andrew Wilson, of course, was deluding himself that he was using such outings as this to assess his compatibility with Miriam. Seldom can such a survey have been less scientific and more blindly pre-ordained. I could only hope that as an adviser to governments he had been less intractably bound to his base-line of prejudice.

That evening he began to talk to me in embarrassing confidence—not asking my advice, except in terms of purely legal procedures—but mainly because Miriam was the only subject that he really wanted to talk about at all. But when he came to his legal queries, I was amazed at the leaps his mind had taken.

In the normal course of events, his sole legatee, except for courtesy bequests, would have been his nephew. If he were to marry again, the conventional solution would be for him to leave his widow a trust income, with the capital protected for the sake of the next generation. But this was hardly likely to be an attractive prospect for Arnold Lowndes; for even if the union did not produce a cousin for him, there was every likelihood that Miriam would survive him. Old Andrew saw this and had been exploring the arithmetic of a proportionate disposition of his fortune, with which he might reasonably expect both parties to be satisfied. He was thoroughly unrealistic about it, and I began to wonder whether I were witnessing the first symptoms of approaching senility. He was genuinely fond of Arnold Lowndes, and at first suggested a settlement in his favour such as would have been resented by any spirited widow; and which showed no expectation of issue from the marriage. And when I mildly pointed this out to him, he swung eagerly in the opposite direction, to the swingeing detriment of his nephew. The accumulation was mostly in funds, with only a domestic holding of real estate. And, really, any division must have left either party in unhappy straits.

'At any rate, Edward, perhaps you'll draw up detailed alternatives for me. I'll let you have facts and figures in a day or two.'

I told him that I would much rather not become involved. He had his own solicitor.

'I shall be living less and less in London. I have been thinking for some time now of putting my affairs entirely in your hands.'

'I really must ask to be excused,' I said.

But Andrew Wilson had a diplomat's way of not taking no for an answer. He clasped his hand over mine.

'Well, don't make your mind up about it now. Give it some more thought.'

He knew that my greatest desire at this particular moment was to leave the subject altogether.

Their next outing was very much more to Miriam's taste. He was going to take her to Manchester, and the implication was that he was going to spend money on her. In this prospect she was prepared to comport herself with grace and patience.

Mabel Mosscrop was by now firmly allied with Andrew Wilson. I think that the 'compensation' of which he had spoken to her had had a great deal to do with this. I do not know exactly what he had proposed, but I have it in my mind somewhere that he was prepared to give her £300, and would go to £500 if necessary: not inconsiderable sums—one might almost call them, in all the circumstances, wildly generous—and which would make a marked temporary difference to Mabel Mosscrop's life-style. There was no strict need, of course, for him to pay anything at all; he was not so much compensating her as buying her support.

But in all fairness to Mabel Mosscrop, I must insist that it was not monetary considerations that weighed solely with her. One of the major sources of difficulty in her life had always been that she was as sentimental as she was mercenary. And the clashes between the two sides in her character sometimes produced some strange rationalisations. She had great power to persuade herself and could sometimes be difficult to dislodge from an illogical course.

She knew that sooner or later she must lose Miriam's services. She knew that this could easily happen in circumstances that might be personally distressing for them all. Miriam was impulsive, and might make irreparable mistakes. In some moods—and there were some differences of opinion between them in which actual physical violence seemed to threaten—she felt that she would be relieved when Miriam finally did go.

But also she felt under a sense of responsibility to the young woman. And Andrew Wilson seemed to her to represent an unimpeachable solution. He was genteel, he was kindly, he was comfortably placed. He had his idiosyncrasies—but what man hadn't?

And Miriam was educable. Had not Mabel Mosscrop herself turned her from a slum child to the princess of the Rose? She was capable of learning from Andrew Wilson, too. Enough to launch her in society in her own right. All she had to do was to be polite and compliant, as she was polite and compliant for nine-tenths of her time in the *Little Rose*. Andrew Wilson was hardly likely to live more than another ten years. She might be free of him in five. True, there might be a few months' incubus of nursing at the end, but there would be money enough to relieve her of the drudgery of it. And at the end of this time, Miriam would still be on the right side of thirty, with her own income, a cultured woman in her own right, with the *entrée* into the circles that mattered.

Mabel Mosscrop began to urge this view on Miriam, I suspect, to nag her about it. By the time the day of the Manchester trip came, she was only too ready for a change of air from the Rose.

She had been to Manchester many times by now, but never before in a first-class compartment; headrests of starched white linen. As Andrew Wilson was helping her over the step, she had the satisfaction of seeing Sam Critchlow pulling himself up from under the platform, where he had jumped down to couple on the engine. He saw her, but made no sign of recognition. And a minute or so later he walked past the window, but with no stronger curiosity than he might have expended on any group of passengers. And yet, for that brief instant when his eye met Miriam's, there was a message for her: it was as if she were one of his own legendary legion of daughters—his very pride.

Miriam was beginning to know the journey very well. Although she considered herself indubitably a town girl, she liked to see the hills above Dove Holes, especially when she was being drawn past them at speed and shielded from their draughts and damps by an adjustable window. But she did not draw Andrew Wilson's attention to the things she saw, as she might have done Mabel Mosscrop's. She knew intuitively that Wilson was above conversing about cows, sheep and foals. Once, indeed, he did drop his paper and gaze vacantly at a hare which their train had started up in a meadow, but he made no comment about it.

Miriam was beginning to understand a number of things that she could not have put into words. She was not familiar with the word *sophistication*—which, indeed, had little vogue in her life-time. But she believed that men (and women) of Andrew Wilson's sort had by some means been born into this world already satiated by its common-places. And she envied them.

Beyond Chapel-en-le-Frith the knolls and tors stretched up towards Kinder.

'I suppose,' Wilson said, 'that this sort of landscape might be said to be your background.'

'I beg your pardon?'

'I'm sorry, my dear. I did not mean to express myself as crudely as that might have seemed. You must know that I would never wish to appear patronising. What I mean is, is this the only type of country that you know?'

'I've been to a lot of other places—Bakewell, Matlock, Castleton...'

'I was thinking of places a little further afield.'

'You mean like Harrogate and Scarborough?'

Jenny Everett had tried her fortunes in both those resorts.

'In Hindustani, the word for *twelve* is *barra*,' Andrew Wilson said enigmatically. 'And they use the same word when they want to say that something is *big*. Because if anything is as far as you can count, it must seem big to you, mustn't it? Italy: now you ought to see Italy.'

'I should love to.'

'Perhaps you will—and before so very long at that.'

At this point Arnold Lowndes interrupted their conversation. He and Annabella Rossiter were travelling with them—perhaps to ensure conventional propriety.

'Miss Bennett, there's a question I've been meaning to ask you arising out of a survey I am conducting amongst my students. You studied History, at school?'

'Romans and things.'

'It seems to have been a comprehensive syllabus. And you found it dull—distasteful?'

'I found *school* distasteful. And I didn't care for History. There's no point in it. History's dead and gone.'

'Out of the mouths...' Andrew Wilson began, but pulled himself up short.

'Precisely, Miss Bennett. And in your heart of hearts, instead of being ashamed of your opinion...'

'Why should I be ashamed of anything?'

'You ought to be proud.'

'What of?'

'Of having enough natural discrimination to find school distasteful and History dull. Because the whole purpose of your schooling was to impress you with a misplaced sense of your own inferiority.'

Andrew Wilson grunted in disgust.

'Instead of which...'

Miriam did not understand what Arnold Lowndes was trying to say. She saw Annabella's eyes fixed on her—erudite, pitying and yet contemptuous, too. She was beginning to dislike this couple very much indeed. Everything they said seemed to be aimed at taking a rise out of her. She was relieved when they had alighted at London Road Station and were heading for the shops.

Andrew Wilson bought her a fifteen carat gold filigree brooch and a length of *Duchesse* flouncing, and also underwrote an account for her at Mabel Mosscrop's favourite milliner's. There was a Princess May bonnet in bright crimson straw which caught her fancy. He also bought her a lady's carriage-bag in green Morocco, which he said she would find invaluable during the weekend in Southport of which he was beginning to talk.

They dined at a hotel which even Mabel Mosscrop would have considered beyond her. Andrew Wilson made great capital out of ordering a *Clos Vougeot* 73.

'Not, I would suppose, a *crû* for which you have much demand in your *Little Rose*?'

'We could get it for you, if you gave us notice,' Miriam said.

She was already aware of the fact that one of the things that appeared to endear her to the toffs was her ability to puncture conceits by down-to-earth rejoinders. And no one could challenge her talent at that.

'*Touché*,' Andrew Wilson said.

And during the course of the meal, an apparently acrimonious discussion arose between Wilson and the other two, in which Miriam began to feel like a conversational shuttlecock.

'A view which no doubt bears the sublime cachet of Owen's College...'

'It has been known as the Victoria University of Manchester since 1880,' Arnold Lowndes said.

'Be that as it may, I still maintain that Whiggery will be providing meat for your dissertations long after your Social Democratic Foundation has become *ancient* history. Miss Bennett, I fear that I have a blood relative who is a Radical.'

'I am sure that Miss Bennett would agree that a wilting stock needs attention at the root.'

'I am sure that she is a respectful traditionalist.'

'And I am sure that she is a democrat,' Arnold Lowndes said.

Miriam could hardly wait to hear Mabel Mosscrop's admiration for the new bonnet.

I was away from Buxton for a few days on professional business at the time of their weekend in Southport, so I cannot provide a first-hand account of the prognostications in the Rose. But I have gathered that Mabel Mosscrop was only partially satisfied by the solidarity of Miriam's attitude. The landlady had had, in fact, to fall back on a half-hearted attempt to persuade herself afresh.

'Well, it's your life. It's up to you what you make of it.'

Which, from Mabel Mosscrop, was almost a forecast of the failure of all her plans.

I am sure that Miriam went to Southport with mixed feelings; but no misgivings actually strong enough to stop her from making the trip. She had never been so far afield; she had never seen the sea before. And experience for its own sake was something that Miriam could seldom resist—provided that it did not threaten to involve her in actual physical discomfort.

Moreover, at this period her working life in the *Little Rose* was at one of its lower ebbs. This came in part from the fact that Mabel Mosscrop was in one of her more easily irritable phases; and this arose in turn, I think, because she was by no means certain in her own mind about the wisdom of the advice she was pressing. The work itself was hard—it always was. The hours were long and this was true even during those periods when life seemed luxurious. If anything was happening behind the scenes to throw the running of the hotel off its even keel—if there was a quarrel with a kitchen-maid, a careless mistake in an order-list, or an unexpected rush of visitors at an hour ear-marked for a free afternoon—then the ordinary tasks of the house became doubly burdensome: the polishing of glasses, the stocking-up of shelves, the fining of ale and the tapping of fresh barrels. Mabel Mosscrop's successful economy depended on her employing fewer hands than she might have paid for—a situation not improved by the fact that Jack did not work at all. And the week before the Southport journey was one of near-catastrophe in the wings, though few of the customers in the front of the house even began to suspect it.

So Miriam Bennett would not have missed the chance of a two day escape at any cost. But already in the train, the less attractive features of the holiday began to obtrude themselves. Andrew Wilson and his nephew began one

of their interminable bickerings. And it all stemmed from
something clever that Annabella Rossiter had said. So the
old man was actually arguing with her through an inter-
mediary.

'You are, I fear, occupying yourself with mere off-shoots
of the essential dichotomy.'

Miriam made a brave effort to interest them in something else. 'Oh, look, the leaves on that tree are beginning
to already turn.'

'To turn already, my dear. Or, already to turn.'

'I beg your pardon?'

'The prime object of language,' Arnold Lowndes said,
hopefully conciliatory, 'is to express meaning.'

My own view is that Andrew Wilson finally lost what
chance he had of her in that moment. He simply could
not wait to attend to her imperfections. Perhaps he even
thought of a propensity to split infinitives as a positive
bar to marriage.

He clearly took a kind of proprietorial right in giving
Miriam her first sight of the sea. He was actually rubbing
his hands in anticipation as they approached the Promenade. But she did not enthuse. The tide was low and far
distant, and the flatness of the beach, its vastness and its
relative freedom from human contamination did not impress her. There were little rowing boats on the Marine
Lake, and she would dearly have liked to go in one of
those; but it was no use asking Wilson to row her; and
she did not relish riding as a passenger alongside Annabella whilst Arnold Lowndes lectured them over the handles
of the oars. She would have liked a ride in one of the
landaus or phaetons in Lord Street. But when she suggested
it, Andrew Wilson appeared not to have heard her; and
he was impatient to walk on when she wanted to look at
the china gew-gaws in the windows of the fancy bazaars
of Chapel Street and London Street. Once, when he had
gone a few yards ahead of her, a gentleman without a

consort raised his hat to her in a frank and open manner that would have been improbable in any of the public places of Buxton.

They walked on the pier and the breeze off the Irish Sea was much stronger than she had expected. It pulled her skirts down about her ankles and filled her face, so that she had to incline her cheek to get her breath. And when they had reached the seaward end, there was no great change in the prospect to reward their effort: sterile, wavy sand beneath them, iron railings on either side, and a floor of even wooden planks, converging in perspective towards the pavilions on the beach. There was nothing to do but walk back, with the wind playing havoc with her coiffure.

As for Annabella and Arnold, being at the seaside did not seem to affect their conception of pleasure. They talked of nothing except the pamphlet that they had written, and into which Arnold wanted to insert some fundamental amendments at proof stage.

'If you are going to say that, you are twisting the man's words,' Annabella said.

'I'm not. I'm editing him.'

'And you call that honest? To say nothing of attracting aspersions on your own scholarship ...'

'But this isn't a work of scholarship.'

'Oh?'

'Not in the sense that it's a source book for posterity. It's meant to be read once, for its immediate impact. So why confuse people with a schism in the opening paragraph?'

In justice to Arnold Lowndes, I do not think that he was ever less than courteous to Miriam. He was never under any illusions about her. But he was too kindly a man ever to want to hurt her feelings. He must have had misgivings about the fate of his inheritance, but he was far too liberal minded, in the truest sense, to want to deprive the old man of a companionship which he so agonisingly needed. I think that if things had gone the way Andrew

180

Wilson wanted, then Arnold Lowndes would have cud-gelled his brains to find a compromise that would have hurt all parties as little as possible. About Annabella Rossiter I am not so sure. I think that beneath the frigid intellectual abstractions which she used as natural camou-flage, there lurked a material selfishness that could win the day in any final confrontation.

At dinner-time that night she was tactless enough—or deliberately mischievous—to try again to educate the old man to her feminist way of thinking.

'Our late Queen,' Andrew Wilson said, not viciously, 'was amused to suggest that young ladies who hold such views deserve to be whipped.'

He turned amiably to Miriam. 'You, at least, my dear, are not politically conscious.'

'I should hope *not*.' She answered in the tone that she might have used in the family circle at the Rose if some-one had tried to bracket her with Kitty Brindley and Annie Brightmore.

Annabella's eyes glistened.

'Perhaps Miss Bennett would care to tell us what, in her eyes, are the advantages to society of a politically un-conscious woman?'

'I wouldn't like you to think that I'm not *conscious*,' Miriam said, hoping that play on a word would be con-sidered witty enough to exhaust the argument. But this did not seem to work. Three pairs of eyes were now wait-ing for a sensible riposte.

'I think it's up to a woman to *be* a woman—to behave like a woman.'

'Bravo!' Andrew Wilson said.

'The two are not mutually exclusive, surely?'

'You mean *Our Mutual Friend*?' Miriam came out with the first silly association of words that came into her head.

'Facetiousness apart . . .' Arnold began.

'I mean, I may not be politically conscious, but I can

181

make a better Yorkshire pudding than the one you've just paid good money for.'

'Bravo!' again.

Now they all laughed; and the subject was dismissed. But when they had finished eating, Miriam and Annabella had to go into the residents' sitting-room whilst the old man and Arnold remained at table over nuts and port. I think it very probable that this was the moment Andrew Wilson had chosen to tell his nephew of his intentions. There was an unusually long interval before they joined the ladies.

And Annabella Rossiter made good use of the time at her disposal.

'You know, Miriam, I find you difficult to understand.'

'There's nothing difficult to understand about *me*.'

'I'm not saying it in any pejorative sense.'

'I don't know what that means.' Already, Miriam was learning how to use her lack of education as a source of sympathetic advantage.

'It means I'm not trying to take a rise out of you.'

'You'd better not.'

'All I'd like to know is, what do you think a woman's role in society should be? What *do* you think women are for?'

Miriam thought seriously for a moment. There seemed to be no harm in provoking this woman. It might be amusing to get her really exasperated.

'To look after men.'

'And to get what you can out of it, while you're about it?'

'I never said that.'

'But it's what you're doing, isn't it, in the case of a man who's sitting not twelve yards the other side of that door?'

'Look: as far as that man is concerned, I started nothing. If he wants to waste his time and money...'

'So how long do you propose to let things go on this way? Are you going to break his heart tomorrow—or next week —or in two years' time?'

'What happens to his heart is his own affair.'

They sat and looked at each other in the silence of loathing for some seconds.

'It's been broken for him once in his lifetime,' Annabella said.

'What do you know about people's hearts, anyway?'

'You see, that's where you make the same ludicrous mistake as everybody else. I don't think it will take him long to get over you, anyway.'

This riled Miriam. It riled her because she felt, even if she did not grasp it in all its refinement, the depth of contempt which it implied. She was still riled when the two men appeared.

She saw Arnold Lowndes signal with a jerk of his head to Annabella and she guessed that the old man wanted the couple out of the way for the next few minutes.

'I hope you'll excuse us, Uncle Andrew. If these galleys aren't ready for tomorrow's first collection...'

'Heaven forfend that I should stand in the way of political subversion. I am sure that Miss Bennett will keep an old man company for the last half-hour of the day.'

Arnold and Annabella left the room, and Miriam stood up and also began to gather her things together. The old man made no effort to keep the disappointment from his face.

'Miss Bennett, I had been hoping...'

She knew that she was about to smite him down with aggressive rudeness. She wanted nothing else.

'I know what you're hoping for. So let me put you out of your misery here and now. You're not going to get it. You might as well start looking elsewhere for it.'

She slammed the door behind her—a gesture in keeping with the finesse of her whole performance. She went up to

183

her room, put on her outdoor coat and floated out past the hall-porter as if she had not seen him.

To get out of here—anywhere; anything to put herself in a different element from these people. To be out in the town, where the lights were shining, where there was music drifting out from the places of public resort.

Across the road from the hotel there sauntered, round-shouldered, a familiar figure. At first she did not believe her eyes. But who else would wear that straw boater at that angle? Who else swing that slender varnished cane? She ran across and seized him by the arm.

'Jonty Bonsall.'

'Miriam.'

'What on earth are you doing here?'

'I came to see you. I want to talk to you. I've got to talk to you. Happen I'm not too late.'

'No my God, Jonty, you're not too late.'

She stood and looked at him in a certain way she had. It was as if she took half a step forward, presenting herself; then half a step backward, in surrender. And yet she appeared not to have moved—not even to have swayed on her feet. Jonty's arms went behind her shoulders. He kissed her as he could hardly have done in any of the public places of Buxton.

Then they walked down to the Promenade. People were just coming out of the Pierrot Show: *Alexander and his Rascals*. Other couples were walking with their arms about each other's waists.

There was a strong breeze blowing in from the Irish Sea, playing havoc with her hair. Dry sand lashed up from the beach stung her cheeks. She did not care.

It was all part of being free.

CHAPTER NINETEEN

When Miriam and Jonty returned to the *Little Rose*, they were in love. Whatever was to happen later between them, there was no doubt about this phase of their lives. They could be seen to be in love, and we wondered sometimes whether they were aware of the existence of anyone but each other. Miriam even went more than once with Jonty to his chapel on the Market Place. For a time she even seemed to beam with a touch of evangelical fervour. It was easy to believe, when the world about her shone with blessings.

Within three months they were married: went for their honeymoon into the Fens, to the cottage of a cousin with whom the Bonsalls had always remained close—a man who carried on the parental trade of painting farmers' wagons. The *Little Rose* gave them a spectacular send-off; and an equally tumultuous welcome home.

Their marriage lasted eight or nine years. So why did it collapse?

I am not competent to answer that. The best I can do is to recall the opinions that I heard people express over the whole period when I was putting together my notes about their history.

Said Joshua Mycock, 'Because he was too bloody decent for her. Because she was nothing but a bloody harlot. As you must have seen with your own eyes. Or perhaps you didn't; perhaps I shouldn't expect you to. No, Mr Bailey: with Miriam Bennett you'd be out of your depth. You'll have to take my word for it. A bloody harlot. That's what she was.'

Said Sam Critchlow, 'I was against it from the start. You

know I was. I never pretended to be otherwise. I'd rather she'd married that other dried-out old weasel. He might have done something with her, but Jonty Bonsall could never have changed her. And I'm not saying that because I can't stand his father. That has nothing to do with it, has it? Any man but Jonathan Bonsall would have aimed at Stanley Redfern below the knees. But I liked young Jonty. I liked both of them. That's why marriage should never have been on the cards.'

'You don't think that Miriam might have moulded him to her image?'

'Jonty Bonsall? He wouldn't give an inch. That's what I'm trying to say.'

Said Jonty's mother, 'I always felt sorry for the girl. I'm sure that life in that hotel was no bed of roses. No, Mr Bailey, I can honestly say I liked her when Jonty first got to know her. She was always so sweet to me when he first started bringing her home. And the girls—our girls, Edith and Martha—they were such friends together at first. They used to love to see her come into the house. She'd been to places that they hadn't.

'Oh, I used to wonder sometimes how she'd settle down on Burbage Edge. I was frightened that Jonty wouldn't earn enough to give her all the things that she'd want to have. But then, they were both working two nights a week at that hotel, weren't they? Of course, I knew that Jonty would never want her to be out working if he wasn't there with her.

'I think that's what worried me most: what Jonty would do if she ever did let him down.'

Said Jonathan, 'It wouldn't have happened if I'd been at home. I'd never have allowed it. I knew the Bennetts, and I never had any room for them. There was rotten blood on both sides.'

'I've heard it rumoured that Bennett was not her father. That Sam Critchlow...'

'That couldn't possibly be true. Sam was away at sea at the time that mattered.'

Said Mabel Mosscrop, 'I had a creeping sort of fear the day Jonty Bonsall first walked into our bar. I had that feeling in my bones, they'd be bad medicine for each other. And yet I suppose I did as much as anybody else to encourage them. You couldn't do otherwise, could you, when you saw which way things were going?

'When he walked in here with her, that Sunday evening, and me thinking she was still in Southport, I could have torn her limb from limb. But then I saw what they meant to each other.

'Of course, we all knew Jonty Bonsall would never make a fortune at the Town Hall. But he'd make a steady income, wouldn't he, and never be likely to get the sack? He was such a decent young man and he thought the world of her. I think that's partly what got her about him: him so decent, and thinking the world of her. Well, your friend Mr Wilson thought the world of her, too, but not in the same way. Not in the same way at all.

'So I said to her, "You'd be a fool if you let him go, Miriam. He won't take you to live in marble halls, but you'll never want for bread and butter. And you can come and earn yourself the odd shilling or two while he's playing the piano. I might see my way to putting that up to three times a week."

'Of course, I knew he'd never let her come here to work if he wasn't on the premises himself. And he was terribly strict with her, you know. Well, he was entitled to be, wasn't he, him being her husband? He used to go through all the house-keeping accounts, same as he would do the books at his office. And he wanted to know where she'd been every minute of the day, even if she'd only been talking to the neighbours. And, I mean to say, Miriam *was* Miriam.

'No. He didn't insist on always taking her to chapel.

187

Well, he didn't keep it up himself, really. I think somebody had said something to him, about playing the piano in here, and he gave up teaching in the Sunday School and all that. But I told her, Mr Bailey, "You'll have to go straight with Jonty Bonsall," not that I think for a minute that she ever did anything to be ashamed of. But he was a terribly jealous man. Perhaps it made him worse because he must have wondered what she was like before he got to know her. Then, on the other hand, he was always such a young innocent, you wouldn't have thought that he'd suspect anything. Not that I'm suggesting there was ever anything to suspect.

'But anyway, they got on all right at first. It ran into years. She used to say to me, when she came here, if she dropped in for a chat between her shopping. "Mabel," she'd say, "I've never given Jonty Bonsall half an ounce of cause for complaint, but sometimes I feel as if I could kick over the traces just because it's all he really expects of me." And I told her she'd be a fool if she ever did.

'And I'm sure she never would have. But then came the morning when Jonty was sent up to one of those cottages in Bishop's Lane, to serve a final notice by hand. And he's only five minutes from home, so he drops in, unexpected. And who should he find in the house with Miriam but Mr Roger Weigall?

'Now I ask you: could it possibly have been Miriam's fault? Is a woman like that going to invite a man to come and see her in her home, with all the neighbours pulling at the curtains? She told me she was flabbergasted when she saw who it was, knocking at the door. And he hadn't been there five minutes when Jonty came in.

'But he wouldn't listen. He wouldn't let her explain. He told her to get out of the house, and she wouldn't, so he said he'd get out himself. And when the next week's rent fell due, she wasn't going to pay it out of her own savings, was she? Why should she? So she came back to live down

188

here. And I didn't like to see them falling apart like that, but the least I could do was to make her feel at home, for old times' sake. Then when it came to suing him for maintenance, I didn't like to see it. Who does like to see old friends going to law? But as I said to her at the time, "If you don't, Miriam, it'll be like admitting that you were in the wrong."

'Besides, I felt certain that Jonty wouldn't keep it up. He'd come round. He'd remember what she used to mean to him.

'We all know he didn't. We all know he wouldn't pay, and they made him do time for it. And we all know what happened after that.'

But there were some things that some of us still did not know.

CHAPTER TWENTY

This time, Inspector Brunt had to wait in the outer office whilst I talked to a client. When I finally asked for him to be brought in, his eyes strayed immediately towards that corner of my desk where my bound manuscript had lain at the time of his previous visit.

I knew that that was what he had come for; but I let him ask for it. As soon as he did, I brought it out of the top drawer and laid it on the desk-top between us. I had no intention of behaving coyly and pretending to withhold it from him. I was proud, in a quiet way, of my modest literary endeavour. What writer does not want his work to be read? And I cannot conceal my hope that I had unwittingly revealed something for which he would be professionally grateful.

'I should like, if I may, to come and see you again in your home.'

'This evening?'

'I cannot be certain of my movements.'

'Come to supper.'

'I certainly could not promise any precise time. It would be as well if you had your meal without me.'

He came, in fact, very late, carrying my manuscript wrapped in an unevenly torn sheet of crumpled brown paper. He laid it down on a side table and I waited for him to refer to it. But evidently he was in no hurry to do so.

This time, he did not object to being divested of his coat. My man had been in twice to keep up an immense fire in the grate, and Brunt would surely have melted like a stub of old candle if he had sat by it in his outdoor clothes.

I thought that there was a strange lack of distance between Brunt and my factotum as the latter showed him in. Neither man revealed whether they had met before or not; but I felt certain that they had. Brunt had been here in my absence and talked to my servant, presumably by the back door and not improbably in his pantry. I felt certain of this; and I resented it. But I said nothing. It seemed stupid to get our conference off on the wrong footing. Besides, I never had been encouraged to think that Brunt was a gentleman.

But he was in a much more expansive, potentially genial mood than I had ever seen him before. I was amazed at the weight of that long coachman's coat as I helped it off his shoulders. The man must have added enormously to his diurnal weariness by bearing such a corpse-like burden everywhere he went. And when he was relieved of it, he must have felt at first as if his shoulders were soaring away to heaven.

He accepted a brandy—which I was sure must be against his departmental rules—and did not look with disquiet at the generous measure which I poured him. Moreover, he clasped his fingers round the glass and savoured the bouquet, not as if it were the ritual which he had seen other men perform, but as if it really meant something to him.

For a few sentences we exchanged generalities—I think we were talking about the brandy itself and I extolled, as I often do, the virtues of Armagnac. Then he set down his glass on the wine table which I had put for him, got up and began to walk about my room, frankly inquisitive. I suppose it had unavoidably become his habit to treat other men's rooms in that way. I felt tempted to go out for five minutes and leave him to it, so that he could see his fill and perhaps become less restless.

But in all conscience, there was nothing offensive in the nature of his curiosity. He picked up a *millefiori* paper-weight by Apsley Pellat: and startled me by knowing that it came from Stourbridge and that French workmen had been employed there. Then he went over to my mantel-piece and looked appraisingly at a miniature which I prize. I suppose that if a man hangs a portrait on a wall of a room into which he invites another, he has no complaint if it is candidly examined.

'Yes,' he said, eventually standing back. 'I can understand why you kept this. What was her name?'

'Elvira.'

'That has a familiar ring about it.'

'Oh,' I said. 'It was a long time after I had given up hope that Andrew Wilson married her.'

'And there came a moment after that when you both knew that all the decisions had been wrong. On the Rigi Kulm . . .'

'The thought was never expressed,' I said. 'It did not have to be.'

'You will forgive my asking you about it. But you did give me your account of it to read.'

'I have no objection to talking about it. I never harboured any bitterness. Elvira was woman enough to be self-sufficient. And Andrew Wilson was always too thick-skinned to be aware of anybody's feelings but his own.'

'You didn't end up with the resolution that you were not going to let him pip you at the post a second time?'

This was so unexpected, so starkly personal and so casually matter-of-fact, that I took several seconds to take it in. At the risk of appearing nervous, I laughed in my throat.

'Good heavens, Inspector—with Miriam, you mean?'

'Again, Mr Bailey, I would hesitate to talk to you like this. But all my thoughts on the subject arise from what you voluntarily gave me to read.'

'You must have misread it, then.'

'I have two things to say about your manuscript, Mr

192

Bailey, and not in the shape of literary criticism. That would not be my sphere at all. But as a working police-man, judging it purely as a possible contribution to detection, I have two things to say.'

'Yes?'

He had gone back to his chair by the fire, and he now held out his hand as if inviting me, if you please, to sit down in my own home. I cannot remember at what point I had stood up; perhaps when he had picked up the paper-weight.

'There is at least one aspect of this affair, Mr Bailey, about which you know too little; another side of things about which you clearly know a good deal too much.'

'How can that possibly be?'

'Southport,' he said briefly. 'You know too much about what went on in Southport.'

'Imagination, Inspector. I would think that all the great detectives succeed only by the skill with which they project themselves into other people's lives.'

But he did not accept the invitation into a backwater.

'In your account of those incidents, Mr Bailey, you mentioned that you were out of Buxton on professional business at the relevant time. Your command of detail is so great that one is tempted to believe that your business took you to Southport.'

'*Histoire romancée*, Inspector. I admit that I took all the pains I could to get the setting right. But that method would be far too risky for a professional investigator. *Histoire romancée* must be the one thing that a policeman most deplores.'

'On the contrary, Mr Bailey. I take your point—about imagination. But how on earth did imagination tell you who were the performers in the Pierrot Show: *Alexander and his Rascals*?'

Again I laughed. 'My word, Inspector, I even seem to have put myself in jeopardy. I told you already: I was determined that the background should be authentic. I consulted newspaper files.'

'So did I. That's how I know that you were right.'

Brunt now looked over the arm of his chair for the wine table and set down his glass from which, in fact, he had drunk very little. He stood up, planted his feet firmly on the hearth-rug and carried out a most peculiar movement, rocking back and forth from his heel to the ball of his foot. He really did look ridiculous, in jacket and trousers that did not belong to the same suit, and a waistcoat that matched neither. Then suddenly he laughed too, spluttered almost apoplectically and flopped back in his chair, still overcome by amusement.

'No, I can't do it, Mr Bailey.'

'Do what, Inspector Brunt?'

'It isn't a skill for which I would have much vocational need, even if I mastered it.'

'*Mastered what?*'

'I was thinking, Mr Bailey, about your remarkably apt description of the stance adopted by Miriam Bennett when she crossed the road from her hotel to confront Jonty Bonsall. Do you know, I believe I could still quote the actual words you used: *half a step forward, presenting herself; then half a step backward in surrender. And yet she appeared not to have moved—not even to have swayed on her feet.* It's very good, that, Mr Bailey. It hits it off absolutely.'

He took the tiniest drop of cognac on the end of his tongue.

'That's just how some of them do carry on. Only I can't manage it. When I try to do it, my body does sway. The art is in simply suggesting movement. Still, every man to his trade, I suppose.'

He clasped his stumpy fingers round the glass again.

'But I'll tell you what I thought, shall I? Only a thought, mind you—I thought, well, it looks to me very much as if Mr Edward Bailey wasn't all that far from the pavement outside that hotel himself. Only, of course, I can't in the least blame him for not wanting to talk about it. Why should he talk about it? It's very much his own personal affair. And probably it wouldn't advance the case in the least. But it would be interesting to know. One of my occupational dangers, the habit of wanting to know everything, even things that don't matter in the least. If Jonty Bonsall, knowing what Andrew Wilson was scheming, knew that this was the crucial evening on which he must talk to Miriam Bennett at all costs, why should the same thought not occur to Mr Edward Bailey? That's how my perverted mind looked at it. Silly of me, I know.'

I did not contradict him. I could feel that my face was flushed, and this made me angry with myself, for he was sure to take it as a symptom of impending confession.

In point of fact, I had been in Southport on the night in question. I had witnessed the meeting between Miriam and Jonty. I had gone there precisely as Inspector Brunt had inferred. I make no effort now to conceal the fact that ten years ago I was, like others, infatuated with Miriam Bennett. It alarms me now to think that I should ever have considered the match possible. And I do not think that I would have stirred in the matter—I would have been content to observe her dreamily from my distant corner—if it had not been for the unexpected competition from Andrew Wilson.

Inspector Brunt's reading between the lines had been surprisingly acute. Why should I cede the day to old Wilson a second time? If he could make Miriam happy in his old age, why could not I? I was ten years younger than him, had so much more to offer her in warmth of humanity, an eye for the little things, a care for nuances. If Andrew Wilson believed that he could smooth off her sharp corners then why could not I, I who would do it with so much more solicitude for her feelings? I who would not allow myself to be jarred by her split infinitives? I who could also afford to buy myself a treaty with Mabel Mosscrop and who could draw up a will unencumbered by entails?

And had I not already had evidence enough that Miriam Bennett did not find me entirely objectionable?

But when I saw the finality of Miriam's and Jonty's embrace, I knew that Andrew Wilson's battle was lost and my own not worth the mounting. Faint heart? A second time in my life, for I knew that it was my own fault that I had had no more of Elvira than her miniature on my wall.

Faint heart? But the lady turned out to be far from fair. I travelled back from Southport alone, feeling more than a bit of a fool. But I joined in the excitement in the *Little Rose* when the other two returned, and for a long time I thought that Miriam had made the right decision.

But I did not confirm Inspector Brunt's sagacity. I did not want to be made a fool all over again.

'And shall I tell you what else I am thinking, Mr Bailey?'

'By all means tell me anything you have on your mind. If I listen patiently, it does not necessarily mean that I am applauding what you say.'

He looked as if he was about to start, and then as if he was going to withdraw from offering this new revelation. But I was beginning to know him well enough to recognise this as a piece of acting—the trick preamble. It became all the more important to say nothing at all: simply listen.

'I'm sorry, sir. It's madness of me to think of talking to you like this. If you were to put in a complaint to my superiors, I would not have a leg to stand on.'

I knew the Chief Constable socially. It was hardly likely, except in very dire straits, that I would want to start from scratch and tell him the improbable story of my imbecility over Miriam.

'Whatever you are thinking, Inspector, I would rather

hear you out than watch it slowly poison you.'

'I'll be honest with you, then, honest about what is only, after all, a theory.'

'Do come to the point, Inspector.'

'I am thinking, sir, about the occasion that you insist on calling the night of Jenny Everett—the night you policed the landing because of Mr Roger Weigall. To my mind, you ought to call it the night of something else. Now tell me, sir, am I right about that?'

Again I felt the hotness in my cheeks, and I knew that it was idiotic of me to let him go on. But it would be disastrous to let him anger me. That is the way we sometimes have with recalcitrant witnesses in court.

'I don't know whether you are right or wrong, because I don't know yet what it is you are trying to say.'

'I am trying to say, Mr Bailey—and remember, this is only theory—that on the night of Jenny Everett, you also saw Miriam Bennett—how shall I put it?—present and surrender. Again, I can quote what you wrote, because it impresses me: "a cambric nightdress with a wide hanging frill. She had let down her hair about her shoulders, and this gave her an elemental look. My head swam..."'

'I think, Inspector, that I have recorded a very honest impression.'

'Indeed you have. An impression that everything seemed to sway. Including Miriam Bennett. Present and surrender. I am tempted to believe that she detained you longer that night than you have in fact recorded.'

I thought he was going to pause for me to answer, but as if on second thoughts he plunged on again before I could say anything. I saw his game. If he could press his story far enough forward with nothing uncontradicted, I had only to confirm some trivial detail in the later stages, and he would have the rest already locked into place. He was an interrogator not to be under-estimated; if he had gone to the bar, he could have made a formidable silk. So

I still suppressed myself. I had to avoid fencing with him. I poured myself another brandy; his was so relatively untouched that I could not offer him more.

'So I said to myself, Mr Bailey, that it must have come as a very bitter shock to you to learn that she opened her door to Mr Roger Weigall later on the very same night.'

'But I've only just discovered that, Inspector. Mabel Mosscrop didn't tell me what she saw until after Miriam Bonsall had been killed.'

'Why do you tell me that?'

'Why do I tell you that? Because it's true.'

'But why are you so keen to tell me that you heard it after she was dead? Do you think that otherwise it would impress me as a motive for killing her?'

'Good God, Inspector, listen to me! You have just made a number of personal and insolent allegations on which I propose to make no comment at all. If I were to confirm every detail of what you are suggesting, it would still not make me the murderer.'

'No. I thought you would have gathered from the tone in which I spoke just now that I would not be satisfied with the motivation that we have so far discussed. But I think you must admit, sir, that we are now on the brink of yet another new and very interesting theory.'

'Are we? I do admit that I am beginning to tire of this nonsense.'

'A pity, sir. I hoped you would hear me out. If I could crave your patience to listen to the whole of my thesis, perhaps you would be able to spot some flaw in it that I can't.'

'I'll listen. But I'll reserve my right to say nothing at all when you've finished.'

He stooped to push back a coal that was leaning out of the fire. He was acting out very well the pose of being nervously embarrassed to be talking to me like this.

'Let us take the hypothesis that after the lamentable

death of Jonty, you returned to the view that you should be the one to take Miriam away from the *Little Rose* as a comfort for your old age.'

He looked at me keenly to see how I was taking it. But I was not blushing now. I am confident that I was showing no reaction at all.

'I admit that it would seem out of character for you, of all men, to make approaches to a widow so impetuously, and so soon after the fateful news. But you were only too well aware, this time, of the penalty for sloth in such matters. Especially when Stephen Stanhope, Arnold Lowndes and Roger Weigall—probably *inter alios*—are in the offing. Why should she not sit on your cushion to sew her fine seam? I quite honestly believe she might have done worse for herself.'

'Thank you very much.'

'Let us say, for the sake of argument, that she has privately told you that you are her favourite. But by some accident you discover that she is still hedging on the field. Now I ask myself what I might feel and do under such circumstances. I am a very placid man. Like you, I am a *moraliste*: I prefer to observe my fellow man, rather than to involve myself personally with him. But now and then I have been unable to avoid some degree of individual commitment. In some ways I fancy—and pride myself—that you and I are very similar men, Mr Bailey. We are both activated by a combination of goodwill, uncomplicated reason and simple justice. And when this is stultified, a momentary loss of temper is an ever present danger. In my case, when this has happened, it is perhaps merely my good fortune that an axe has not been lying conveniently handy.'

A massive, stilted and phenomenally careful speech. He paused to examine its effect on me. I did my best not to gratify him. So he continued.

'So I tell myself that in such complex circumstances, to undertake the defence of Jonathan Bonsall would be a concluding subtlety that I can only stand back and admire.'

'Arrant nonsense!' I said, in spite of my resolve to give him nothing at all. He then reverted to the eccentricity of our first meeting and said nothing for a very long time.

'And have you outlined this theory to your superiors?' I asked him, thinking that I might have to seek an audience with the Chief Constable after all.

'Indeed I have.'

'And yet they maintain you in office?'

He brushed this aside with a cloud across his expression which suggested that he was disappointed that I should sink to such depths.

'It was suggested that such a theory would require substantial reinforcement.'

'I see some hope for law and order in this country after all.'

'And therefore I must tell you, Mr Bailey, that the prospects for Jonathan Bonsall now look very black indeed. It seems even probable that I am about to be moved to some new and distant case, since it is now considered that I have wasted more than sufficient time on this one.'

So now what was he getting at? He did not bear the look of a man who had yet finished all he had come here to say.

'There is a further circumstance, Mr Bailey, that lends some support to my theorising—albeit inconclusively.'

'Oh? And what is that?'

'That you can scarcely be said to have pursued your client's interests with due diligence.'

This was meant to be a belly-blow; and it very nearly was. He very nearly had me off my balance, which is what he was aiming for. I could feel my blood-pressure rising, although I managed to answer in a frigid tone.

'I wish you would be more precise, Mr Brunt.'

'There is more than one obvious aspect of this case which

200

you have neglected. Perhaps I have mistaken your motives for doing so.'

'But clearly you have neglected nothing, Inspector. So if we were to pool our findings ...'

'Ah!' he said. 'No, sir. No, sir. That would not do at all. I think we must arrive independently at the same conclusions.'

CHAPTER TWENTY-ONE

Inspector Brunt left me shortly after that. And it is true that I was guilty of some of the deceptions and peccadilloes that had come to light in my long conversation with him, but I was not in a hothouse mood of introspective remorse. I merely reflected that if there is a greater moral turpitude than to have wasted one's life, then I am innocent of it.

The reason for my disquiet was much more material. Inspector Brunt could not sincerely believe that I had murdered Miriam, but he did think that perhaps I might have done. The situation would have been so very simple if I could have shown in a simple statement that I had been nowhere near the *Little Rose* at the time of the killing.

But the obvious truth was not on my side. The yard of the Rose, with its ungated lane from the Station. Approach, was ludicrously accessible. The whole terrible incident had taken place within a few violent seconds in the late afternoon. And I could not say exactly where I had been at that specific time—I did not even know what the specific time was. I only knew that within that hour I had left my office, had been to a stationer's shop and a tobacconist's and had then walked in a leisurely fashion back home. I could easily have been the one who had slipped down the lane and into the yard. It was quite useless trying to pretend otherwise.

But if I were the murderer, then as Inspector Brunt had said, it might have been an act of consummate subtlety to have come forward, at my own expense, to take charge of Jonathan's defence; especially if that defence were to devolve into an otiose gesture, which it certainly would be if Brunt was now withdrawn and the case allowed to drift along its present course.

So it now behoved me to throw a welter of energy into Jonathan's cause, if only to show my own *bona fides*. But there was another, and even more urgent reason for my doing so: I did believe in his innocence.

Knowing that I would not sleep, and dreading the *perpetuum mobile* of lying awake in darkness, I put on my outdoor things and walked for an hour and a half about the town and its outskirts. A foolish thing to do. If anyone had seen me, my motives, if not my sanity, would have been suspect. If Inspector Brunt had it in a patch of his devious mind that I might be the killer, then there would be others who would have gossiped each other independently into the same belief. But I met no one; Buxton slept. I caught sight of a beat constable in the distance, but I was able to evade him.

I passed the *Little Rose*: curtains drawn, blank windows that told no tale. I climbed the Station Approach, looked down into the inn yard: no ideas latent there. I could not induce a *frisson* in my veins. Up past the railway station, over Palace Fields; a rattle of couplings in the goodsyard: Sam Critchlow on night duty? I skirted Hogshaw, where he had once rescued Miriam from the *émeute* of enraged viragoes.

I have mentioned that I am a lazy man: but the quality of laziness is not just a matter of steering clear of physical effort. It is an evasion of inimical issues. As Jonathan's representative I had been negligent almost to the point of torpor. I had shirked the rigorous mental discipline that might have extracted something from timings and movements about the inn yard; it was probably too late now. I could have engaged some shifty agent to make inquiries about comings and goings up the Station Approach; but no one would remember anything now. I could have had questions asked—perhaps asked them myself—about Stephen Stanhope, Roger Weigall and company. Presumably Inspector Brunt had done this; but there are some men who would rather not tell a policeman anything.

Coming back into town, turning my footsteps towards home, deciding that it had to be bed after all, I saw that there was one possibly useful move that I could still make. Tomorrow morning I would go and see Arnold Lowndes.

He received me in the little room in which he conducted seminars in his Victoria University. He had put on some weight since I had last seen him a decade or so ago; was more mature and more harassed. I asked after Andrew Wilson's health.

'Not quite bed-ridden. But I don't know how he'll weather another winter.'

'He must have been very disturbed by what happened a few years ago.'

Arnold Lowndes looked at me as if he would have preferred me not to have resurrected the subject. I wondered whether he had by now married Annabella Rossiter or whether it would be better not to ask after her.

'He never said a word to me of what he felt. Whatever harm it did him, it remained inside.'

Arnold Lowndes did not want to talk about it. I had always like this man; but he gave no appearance of being glad to see me now. Perhaps I was making him late for some appointment that he was too polite to mention.

'What *do* you wish to see me about?'

'You know what's been going on in Buxton?'

'I've been told to expect a *sub poena* as a prosecution witness.'

Which could be an effective bar to anything I might learn from him now. My eyes wandered round the room. His books: Lovett's *Life and Struggle*; Samuel Bamford's *Passages*; Maitland's *English Law and the Renaissance*.

There was so much that this young scholar and I could have in common.

'I saw a copy of your disposition at the committal,' I said. 'Your evidence will purely be a few simple questions of time and place. I wondered whether the police have interviewed you on wider issues.'

'If they have, it is a matter of confidence between themselves and me.'

'I don't challenge that,' I said, and lined up my gloves on a couple of books I had bought on my way out along the Oxford Road.

'What's your interest, anyway?' he asked.

'I'm defending Jonathan Bonsall. Did you ever meet him?'

'I've heard of him. I saw him for three minutes in the *Little Rose*. A ruffian, by all accounts.'

'If you knew him, you'd qualify that.'

'I don't see that there's any help I can give you. I saw Bonsall walk into the bar that afternoon. I heard him ask Mrs Mosscrop if he could see his daughter-in-law. I saw him go out into the yard. I observed the consternation that followed. That is all.'

'Did Inspector Brunt ask you what you were doing in the *Little Rose* in the first instance?'

'I told him the truth about that. I had come to make arrangements for a series of evening lectures.'

'You were in company with a Mr Weigall?'

'A chance meeting.'

'I am sure that Brunt did not believe that.'

'Mr Bailey, you were at one time a close friend of my uncle. If I thought that our private, family business would help, I would have no objection to its seeping into court. But . . .'

'My client wishes he had not to go into court at all.'

'I've no doubt he does.'

'I've asked you what you were doing in the *Little Rose*

with a Mr Roger Weigall. If you feel you cannot tell me now, I will make sure that learned counsel worms it out of you, under the vigilance of the judge. But let me not rely on a mere threat of personal embarrassment. You saw Jonathan Bonsall for three minutes in the bar. Describe your unprejudiced impression of him.'

Arnold Lowndes shrugged his shoulders.

'A nonentity. He stood there, ill at ease. Not knowing where to put himself, I believe that is the phrase.'

'Exactly. And you'd see him hang? To protect you and your uncle from ephemeral publicity? Is that the new liberalism?'

He looked past me at a pile of papers on his desk. They had been under his eyes all morning. I was sure they were not inspiring him now.

'All right, I'll tell you. I'll telescope the story; because you'll quickly see that it is a waste of your time. There was a man called Stephen Stanhope, a young dilettante.'

'I met him.'

'I did not hear of him until Roger Weigall told me the whole story. Stanhope used to take Miriam Bennett on so-called geological jaunts. He fell under her spell and made a proposal of marriage to her. His parents intervened and an attempt was made to buy her off. She refused a settlement in a fit of pique.'

'I remember.'

'It seems that Miriam's husband kept her short of money. At least, in view of her tastes in clothes alone, she must have been short of it. She hit upon the idea—and to my mind someone may have been advising her—of an attempt at blackmail. Stanhope had just become engaged to a rear-admiral's daughter and Miriam threatened to write to the fiancée. Whether the girl would have sent back the ring, I don't know, but there would have been some embarrassing scenes, and Stanhope took fright. He came to see Miriam and ran into Weigall. She had been threatening to write to Weigall's wife, too; but Weigall had settled for the paradoxical alternative of accepting further services from her at an inflated rate. Then she wrote to my uncle, threatening no more than to become a nuisance to him. I took the handling of it out of his hands. I went to Buxton, intending to settle Miriam's hash, and put her in the hands of the police if necessary. That was when I ran into Weigall. He was on a similar errand. She had started playing it both ways with him again, and he had had enough.'

'And I've no doubt that you and Weigall can give each other the perfect alibi?'

'And an honest one at that.'

'Tell me.'

'All right. I will. It makes no odds. I'd had the good fortune to eavesdrop on Miriam and Weigall that morning. He had paid her all he was going to, for past, present or future. I buttonholed him in the bar, introduced myself, told him my mission. We would make a joint approach to her; enough bluff from such an unexpected alliance, and perhaps we would not need the police.'

'Had you had the chance to confront her before she was killed?'

'We had. In the bar. After lunch.'

'How did she take it?'

'Petulantly. She flounced out of the bar and up the stairs. But she knew the game was finished. That was all that interested us.'

'That was the last time you saw her alive?'

'It was. At roughly a quarter to four, if you want chapter and verse.'

'But she must have come down again, and out into the yard?'

'Which she could easily have done without our knowledge.'

'Neither of you went out there?'

'No. Brunt has cross-checked that. We sat together, finishing the drinks we had in front of us. We had little in common, and our business was finished. I had one eye on the clock, and I proposed to leave at a quarter past four.'

'Was Mabel Mosscrop about during this time?'

'She was working in the scullery with the door open, so that she could hear if any customer came in. Sam Critchlow turned up a few minutes after four.'

'Just a moment. Which way did he come in?'

'The back way. He behaved as if he were one of the hotel staff, rather than a member of the public. Then the landlord showed up, he seemed to have been in bed till now. He looked a terrible wreck. Tie loose round his neck and even his waistcoat unbuttoned. And that was the moment Bonsall came in.'

'Through the street door?'

'That's right. Jack Mosscrop called to his wife, but before she could attend to Bonsall, she had to tidy up her husband's clothing.'

'How did she behave towards him?'

'She was annoyed. She pulled him about like an old sack. Then she spoke to Bonsall and went upstairs. I don't know whether she really intended to bring Miriam down, or was merely humouring him. As I've said, Bonsall stood there uncertainly for a minute, then went out through the back. It doesn't eliminate Bonsall, does it?'

'No. But it opens up the field to a number of others. It makes me curious about Sam Critchlow. But we needn't assume, need we, that the murderer ever entered the hotel at all. Perhaps he came no further than the yard.'

I decided to put on a display of absolute frankness with young Lowndes. It might be the final touch that would win his co-operation.

'I could have come into the yard myself,' I said. 'And if I were accused, I could not account satisfactorily for my movements.'

'But in your case, there would be no semblance of a motive.'

'Wouldn't there? Perhaps I should tell you that at one time I was at least as foolish over Miriam Bennett as your uncle was.'

'And she was trying to blackmail you, too?'

'No. I think that would have been too risky. I am too close to the doorstep.'

'Excuse me.'

Lowndes had heard movement in the corridor outside his door. A group of his students was queuing up to see him. I heard him make a later appointment with them.

'So in point of fact,' I said, when he returned, 'your evidence is only likely to be used to support the case against Jonathan.'

'Essentially, I suppose. But only insofar as it confirms his statements about his own movements. And he *was* holding the axe, wasn't he?'

I suddenly felt that it would cost too much effort to say anything else about Jonathan and the axe. So it was stalemate. Then, to my relief, I saw that Lowndes was prepared to try once more.

'I doubt whether it will help. But let's try a hypothesis, shall we? Let's work out a case against Critchlow.'

He began to count off points on his fingers. 'One: Critchlow's a rogue. Two: Critchlow's probably the catalyst behind Miriam's blackmail, which is what Weigall certainly thinks. Three: Critchlow has access to Miriam's favours if ever they are not more profitably engaged...'

'Now, steady,' I said. 'I don't think I've ever heard so much to debate in one statement in my life.'

He looked at me in surprise. 'Is it Critchlow you're defending now, then? Well, all right; you be *advocatus diaboli*. I'll take it a point at a time. Critchlow's a rogue. Weigall was so convinced that he was the real force behind Miriam, that he had set a private inquiry agent on to him. And for one thing, Critchlow never set foot on ship-board in his life.'

'But it's a local legend.'

'Exactly. Legend's the word. According to Weigall's in-formant, Critchlow left home thirty years ago to go to sea. He made his way from Buxton to Chatham and was turned down by the doctors. He took a lad's job in the railway yards in North London somewhere, and lodged in Kentish Town. He came back here in his early forties in a seaman's guernsey with an anchor tattooed on his forearm and a string of tales about a daughter in every port.'

'It's going to take me a little while to recover from this.'

'Yes, well, I noticed years ago, when I was staying in Buxton with my uncle: there were quite a number of you only too ready to give Sam Critchlow encouragement. A man like that can be an amenity in a bar.'

'What you are saying is possible. And I have no doubt that Weigall's man did his homework. But I find it diffi-cult to believe that Sam Critchlow's relationship with Miriam . . .'

'I don't find it difficult to accept any man's relationship with Miriam.'

'But there's even a school of thought that called him her father.'

'Well, if Sam Critchlow was her father, the situation sur-passes the pale. I was in the *Little Rose* the night before Miriam was killed.'

'I didn't see you there.'

'I arrived very late, by the last train from Manchester, and I stayed in my room. Miriam showed me upstairs and evidently assumed that I had come to do business with her—blackmail business. I told her that I would want to talk to her in the morning. I was feeling pretty tired, and not enjoying the prospect of the show-down. She brought me a clean towel, loitered a few seconds in my open door.

I think it was probably a habit with her to see whether there might be anything doing, at any time of night or day. Then when I started to close the door myself, not caring whether I knocked her down with it, she tripped off downstairs. Two minutes later I came out to wash my hands, and I looked over the banister and caught sight of her and Critchlow, passing each other on one of the lower corridors. They didn't hug and kiss each other, or anything like that. It was the way they looked at each other, the way they trailed hands as they passed, the way she backed into a doorway to give him room without giving him room. There was nothing of father and daughter about it. Oh, I'll admit that when I was in Buxton before, the year of that fiasco in Southport, his attitude to her was paternalistic. But so was his attitude to all the other girls he talked about, those who existed only in his imagination.'

Arnold Lowndes perhaps did not know how much he was telling me.

'A lonely man, Mr Bailey. A bachelor. A man who knows how to make an audience laugh. Some men do it on the stage for a living. Some men do it in their private lives because it gives them a circle of company. They can do it so long that it becomes part of their character. I'm not a psychologist. I don't know all the jargon that they use these days. But I believe that paternalism was also part of his act. It was something he needed. A man who needed to be a father.'

I took my time in answering. I was no longer *advocatus diaboli*. I knew too well. Had I not at one time suspected that Sam Critchlow might be grooming the girl for his own future needs, perhaps unconsciously? Had not I always felt that she had previously been too immature for him? That he would prefer a matron to a slip of a girl? An Amazon like Mabel Mosscrop, whose glories were surely beginning to fade?

'Mr Lowndes, you will have to authorise me to tell Inspector Brunt...'

'Tell him what you like. Let's get at the truth and have done with it.'

Yet even at that, Brunt showed himself a sharper man than me.

CHAPTER TWENTY-TWO

My inquiries for the whereabouts of Inspector Brunt met with gloomy doubts, both in the Buxton Police Station and at his county headquarters. He had gone to investigate a killing, primeval in its emotional motivation, in a mining village somewhere between Chesterfield and Clay Cross. But I must say that for a man who was risking his sartorial elegance at the coalface, he appeared in my office with remarkable speed.

He dabbed his eyes, once and for all. For the remainder of the time that he spent in my company, his pupils rested on those about him with very steady clarity.

'So you think that perhaps Mr Samuel Critchlow . . .'

'Deserves a few more minutes of your attention.'

'Well,' he said. 'At least we know where to find him.'

'*We?*'

'I would like you to come with me. To prompt my memory, should I ask for your assistance. I would prefer you to say nothing unless I invite you to.'

And it was only at this point that I felt certain that he had previously known nothing at all about the blackmail angle; that Arnold Lowndes had breathed no word of it to him, hoping for his uncle to be left in peace for his last few months. And I flattered myself that he had pushed me into my further inquiries in order to see what I might uncover.

As we approached the *Little Rose* together, I felt his shoulder bump into mine.

'We will go in by the back way, I think.'

So it was up Station Approach and down the lane. And when we approached the spot where Miriam had died, I felt his footsteps begin to drag. Before us lay the rectangle of light from the scullery window. To our right, indiscernible in the shadows, the very area in which her body had lain. I had no eerie feelings now. But it was a sober moment, knowing as much for certain as I now knew about Miriam Bennett.

'Mr Bailey, if I might ask you...'

He was indicating the direction of the shed door, behind which the effects of Miriam and Jonty lay stored.

'Surely, yourself...' I started.

'No. I would not have the right. I have no warrant.'

And he drew something out of his pocket and handed it to me. 'A new contrivance. A hand-lamp, powered by the generation of acetylene gas. We are trying them out in the force.'

So he was here without a warrant. And he was worried by the possible outcome of failure. It made me think that perhaps after all he had not been entirely acting when he had said that his superiors had taken him off the case.

'Go on!' he said. 'It would be better for me not to go in there. Whereas no one can possibly harm you. I will guarantee that no one will interrupt you. I am not in a position to detain anyone yet. But I don't doubt that I can keep them talking.'

'And what am I looking for?'

'Letters. Particularly drafts of letters. Particularly drafts of blackmail letters. I think it unlikely that anything will have been kept. But it would be lunacy not to look.'

I pushed open the shed door and went in and closed it behind me. Inspector Brunt stepped backwards into the shadows.

The *jardinière* on the chest of drawers: I opened one or two of them. They were tightly packed with bed linen and table cloths, and other objects that did not belong there, evidently pushed in by the carrier in his haste: kitchen ladles, wooden spoons, wall pictures and a flatiron. Here was the museum of the young couple's earlier aspirations, but no letters. There was a family bible, and inside it a note, pressed between frontispiece and fly-leaf: but it was only a consolation from someone, a stranger to me, to Jonty's grandmother on the death of her husband.

In a corner, wedged amongst the legs of a pair of stacked kitchen chairs, was the lady's carriage-bag in green Morocco that Andrew Wilson had bought for Miriam in Manchester. I had to stand on a stool to reach it down. It contained one object only: a *fichu* neckerchief of a colour that would have eluded me under the artificial torch-light. But I knew that it was turquoise. She had worn it that night in South-port, as she had walked across the road to present herself to Jonty.

This was no place for me. It was no occupation after my heart to be fishing about amongst these intimacies. And there would be no incriminating correspondence here. If Sam Critchlow had had anything to do with the black-mail, he would surely have seen to that. So what was Inspector Brunt playing at, isolating me in here?

Testing, on this final run, whether I might be frightened out of my wits by my proximity to the scene of a crime which he still thought I might have committed? Or simply ensuring that I was out from under his heels for ten vital minutes, and yet on call if he needed me?

I came back into the yard, and could not see him. I called softly into the shadow into which I had last seen him disappear, and he did not come out of it. The light was still shining in the scullery window and the back door was just off the latch. I knew that that was a signal to me. He had gone into the house.

I went in by the door we always used when we came back in from the yard. In the scullery a tap was dripping in an enamel bowl. I listened for the inherent murmur that was the descant of the *Little Rose*. But the house was strangely silent. I pushed open the door that brought me in beside the bar counter. And except for three people, the room was deserted. I do not know whether Brunt had asked the other guests to go, or whether out of some unerring crowd instinct they had read his purpose as he came in, and quietly got up and left.

Brunt, Critchlow and Mabel Mosscrop were sitting at separate tables, a long way apart. It was unusual for Critchlow to be anywhere but at his corner of the table. Mabel Mosscrop had one elbow on the table and was resting her forehead on her hand. It was not normally her way to relax from conscious poise. I did not see at once, though I noticed a moment or two later, that she had been crying.

'You'll have to find a better tale than that to tell to Tom Brunt.'

'I've told you, haven't I, I've not set foot in Number Three shed for donkey's years.'

Sam Critchlow's exasperation was not that of a man who has been startlingly accused of murder. It was the anger of one who is being unjustly pestered with a triviality. Brunt fumbled with the pages of an incredibly tattered notebook, interleaved with folded papers in all manner of disintegration.

'Well, let's just try to straighten this out, then. This wagon is supposed to have come down coupled to a goods-and-passenger from Stockport on the Tuesday evening. It was shunted into the Ashbourne siding, and then went to the Silverlands yard to await make-up of the night train. So who uncoupled it before the Stockport coaches were backed out for cleaning? You?'

'God Almighty, Inspector Brunt, why do you come to me about it? There's some of those bloody Irishmen in that Bridge Street warehouse.'

'Because once they've got their knife into a man, these people can't leave anyone alone.'

This was Mabel Mosscrop, lashing out with all her rage against the nearest target.

'What would I want to steal a basket of bloody racing pigeons for?'

Sam Critchlow was in the almost witless panic of a man who firmly believed that if Brunt chose to press a charge about a consignment of birds, then he would make that charge stick, even if there was not a shred of justification for it.

'What would I want with racing pigeons? You'd only have to open the lid and the buggers would be off home, wouldn't they?'

'I don't know why you can't get on with the things that matter,' Mabel Mosscrop said.

'Oh, yes? What things are those then?'

'You know very well what I'm talking about.'

'I will if you tell me.'

Mabel looked at him with tightened indrawn lips. Brunt twisted round to catch Sam Critchlow's eye with a mystified look, as if suddenly appealing for rational male support. He was entirely ignoring my existence.

'Easy, now, Mabel,' Critchlow said. 'This other business will clear itself up. The Inspector and I . . .'

But Brunt did not propose to let the other matter drop. 'Now this other thing, Mrs Mosscrop, you weren't by any chance still thinking of Mrs Miriam Bonsall?'

'Who else are we thinking about, every waking and sleeping moment?'

'Yes. Especially waking, I would imagine'—this said almost as an aside. 'Well, Mrs Mosscrop, if you have anything to add on that subject, I shall be only too happy to pay attention. But I thought that you two were quite content to wait for Jonathan Bonsall to swing into space.'

'I don't like Jonathan Bonsall,' Sam Critchlow began, following his usual line. 'But . . .'

'But we all want to be fair. All right, so let's be fair then.'

And at this point Brunt got up, stood in front of the

other two in a space clear of chairs and tables and began rocking from his heel to the ball of his foot, exactly as he had done up in my room. Only now he looked a good deal more ludicrous; partly because his long coat was trailing open behind him, its hem dragging on the ground when he sagged at the knees; and partly because he was doing all he could to appear ridiculous.

Mabel Mosscrop turned to me in appeal. 'Is this man mad, Mr Bailey?'

Clueless, I was about to frame some sort of reply: *I don't think so*—but Brunt took the stage again, coming to rest on his feet and panting a little.

'No. It's no use. I can't do it.'

'Can't do *what*, Inspector Brunt?'

He subsided into the nearest chair and threw the initiative to me. 'You explain to them, Mr Bailey. It was your observation that put me on to it.'

It was one of the most difficult explanations that I ever had to make.

'It's a sort of gesture,' I said. 'A caricature. A way Miriam Bonsall had of—'

'A caricature? Of Miriam Bonsall? I must say, there's a time and place for everything...'

'I wouldn't have thought you were still worried by the finer points, Mrs Mosscrop.' I was relieved to see Brunt taking charge of the talk again. 'Let me put it as concisely and as unemotionally as I can. It was a way Mrs Bonsall had of standing, when she was in a certain situation. I am indebted to Mr Bailey, because he hit it off exactly. *Present and surrender.* It was a way Miriam Bonsall had of looking at a man. I'm quite sure you're both familiar with it. And she did it without seeming to sway on her feet. You saw it, didn't you, Sam—perhaps on more than one occasion—but certainly on the afternoon you came down through the yard on the day after Jonty had died. Because she'd been watching for you, hadn't she? Because things had come to a completely different pass between you and Miriam, hadn't they, during this last year or so? Now Jonty was dead, and there was no obstacle between you at all. You'd even suggested that a little bold blackmail might start you off with a useful little nest-egg, but you hadn't thought that things were going to drop so neatly into your hands as by Jonty dying. However, that's neither here nor there. She could hardly throw her arms round your neck as you came down the lane; not in full view of the scullery window. But she could look at you, couldn't she, in the way she had?'

Brunt paused; he was not wanting answers to his questions yet. 'Simpering, wasn't she? So you came past her, and in through the back door. But you'd seen it, too, hadn't you, Mrs Mosscrop? You knew what that look meant. Was that the first intimation that you'd had? Or was it the final confirmation of something you'd been suspecting ever since she came back to live down here? And after all those years of waiting for Sam! You rushed out and into the shed. Some people would argue that an axe isn't a woman's weapon; but, do you know, I almost think I know how you felt. No wonder you were a bit rough with Jack's collar and tie. And there was Jonathan Bonsall, waiting to walk into it.'

But Sam Critchlow was on his feet.

'You bad bitch!'

'Mabel Mosscrop, I am arresting you ...'

'I'm saying nothing,' she said.

CHAPTER TWENTY-THREE

Histoire romancée...

I cannot describe the homeward journey of Jonathan and Alice. I was not there to see it; I can only think about it. I hope that they did not have to wait for too long on a platform at Derby Station, in full view of the waiting-room where the misguided porter had tried to help. Perhaps they found a cup of thick, sweet tea at some café in the forecourt, and could delay their entrance until the train was about to leave.

Their feelings must have been in a tangle. But for all their vicissitudes, they still meant a good deal to each other, those two. I like to think that some sort of promise of peace settled round them as they saw again the scree-covered hills, pulled out of Monsal Head tunnel on to John Ruskin's viaduct.

I did not see very much of them in the ensuing years. I had an extended stay on the continent, at Baden-Baden, at my favourite, less populated spa: Aix-la-Chapelle. I prefer the French name.

I hardly think that they would walk home down the Station Approach. There is a slightly longer way, by which they could avoid any sight of the *Little Rose*.

I hope that, despite their bitterness and poverty, they were able to derive something from their next few years. This was the late spring of 1911. There were little more than three years left of the Buxton that we had loved.